Prip' יat

The Beast of Chernobyl

Mike Kraus

To My Readers:

Thank you for taking this journey with me.
Without your support, the books I write would not be possible.
Thank you.

Sincerely,
Mike Kraus

Prip'Yat: The Beast of Chernobyl

Introduction

On April 26, 1986, at approximately 1:23 AM Moscow time, reactor number four of the Chernobyl nuclear power plant exploded. The explosion was devastating enough that it utterly destroyed the reactor casing and caused chains of explosions throughout the building, decimating all hopes of containment. When compared with the radioactive material released by the bombing of Hiroshima, Japan, the explosion at Chernobyl released four hundred times more radioactive material into the atmosphere.

Caused by a critical overload of the reactor core due in part to human error and design flaws, the Chernobyl accident was by far the largest nuclear power disaster in history. Direct death estimates from the explosion and short-term extreme radiation exposure range from thirty-one to sixty-four, with tens of thousands more expected to die from cancer caused by exposure to radiation. These individuals include workers at the plant at the time of the explosion and residents of the nearby city of Prip'Yat, located just a few kilometers from Chernobyl.

Designed and built as a home for the thousands of workers at the Chernobyl nuclear power plant, Prip'Yat stands as one of the foremost examples of a true ghost town on the planet. The initial evacuation did not start until the day after the disaster, after many residents were already experiencing symptoms of severe radiation exposure. Buses arrived and evacuated the fifty thousand residents over a period of just a few hours on April 27. The evacuation was only supposed to be temporary at first as the authorities tried to downplay the severity of the explosion. It quickly became apparent that the situation was more serious, though, and the evacuation became permanent.

Because the evacuation was originally only supposed to last for a few days, most residents left all of their personal belongings in their homes. Traces of these belongings still exist throughout the city to this day. A great deal of the area has been torn apart and stolen away by thieves and vandals, but most of it still stands as a contaminated monument to the scale of the disaster.

Prip'Yat has also stood as a source of fear, inspiring stories that tell of mutants, ghosts, and the undead that still walk its streets. A combination of radiation, animal mutations, nearby deaths, and the restlessness of the human imagination all fuel these rumors. Overnight journeys into the city are prohibited and daytime tours are limited in duration to protect visitors.

Officially, the reasons for these prohibitions are to prevent tourists from being exposed to radiation and the danger of collapsing buildings.

Unofficially, rumors are still spoken about the monsters of Prip'Yat that supposedly roam the streets at night, preying on the few unfortunates who dare trespass on their domain. Of the few vagabonds and miscreants who have entered the city under the cover of darkness to steal what valuables still remain, few ever make a second trip. Their stories are not easily extracted, and they spend the rest of their days living in mortal fear of the darkness. Whether they are better off or worse off than the ones who never return from the city, though, is up for debate.

Chapter One
Yuri Volkov | Dimitri Alexeiev

Dimitri and Yuri hurried through the woods, using the cover of twilight to advance. Their flashlights were off and their skin was covered with dark clothing, hiding all but their hands and faces. They whispered to each other as they knelt in the soft grass, catching their breath as their pants were dampened by the dew on the ground.

"We need to move, Dimitri. The air in this field is foul and I swear that I can feel the radiation seeping into my bones!"

Dimitri punched his younger cousin lightly in the shoulder and whispered in return. "Will you shut up already? You're always going on about the doom and gloom, never positive about anything! We'll be just fine. Check your radiation meter and let's get going."

Yuri looked down at his chest, verifying that his disposable radiation measurement tag was still within the safe levels. He shook his head as Dimitri sprinted off, wishing that he had never listened to his cousin. It was Dimitri's idea to go on this silly trip, of course. Everything they did was Dimitri's idea. This adventure was so much more different than the others, though. Their parents thought they were at a school camp, gone for three nights, when they were actually sneaking through a forbidden forest and past military checkpoints.

Come on cousin! It'll be fun! We'll camp for one night and be back home before anyone thinks to check with the school! Dimitri's confident voice still rung in Yuri's ears as he ran after his cousin, bounding through the thick grass of the open field just past the wooded area.

Prip'Yat had been abandoned for years, but there were always stories and rumors, urban legends of people who had stayed past the evacuation, living with the radiation until it changed them, mutating them into something both less and more than human. For the two cousins, it had always been a source of midnight whisperings and late night talk about what creatures could be lurking in the dark, waiting to feast upon any travelers who ventured too far into the Exclusion Zone.

The stories were all myths, or so people had insisted. Tourists had been traveling into the Exclusion Zone for years, starting in 2002 after the government decided that the city's radiation levels were low enough that it could be opened for tourism purposes. Tour operators popped up all throughout Kiev once this policy was put into place, and within a few years hundreds of tourists were traveling back and forth to Prip'Yat, gazing upon the city frozen irrevocably in time.

The boys were not convinced, though. The rumors had still persisted. Every tourist who was injured, every mysterious sighting and every disappearing face in a window all served to fuel the boys' imaginations. Once they grew to be seventeen and eighteen, most of their peers had moved on from the stories of Prip'Yat, focusing instead on girls and vodka, but Dimitri and Yuri continued to be fascinated. Every night they would meet at one of their families' homes, whispering late into the night about new things they had found out about the city, both real and imagined.

The arrival of the chance to see Prip'Yat by themselves without being burdened by a tour group came in the early fall, when their school traditionally held camping retreats for the students. Dimitri and Yuri found out that the retreats in the final year of school had been canceled, but their parents hadn't been informed, and were fully expecting their children to attend camp just like they always had. Seizing this opportunity, Dimitri spent a full week convincing Yuri to travel with him into the Exclusion Zone, taking an overnight trip into a place they had spent most of their childhood dreaming about.

Residents who grew up in the cities near Prip'Yat were not often the ones to visit. In fact, Dimitri and Yuri's parents were strongly opposed to the idea of venturing into the area, thinking it foolhardy that anyone would wish to put themselves in danger by traveling to such a place. Radiation was not the only danger, after all. Wild animals, buildings in danger of collapse and the checkpoints full of guards with itchy trigger fingers were all a concern. A full week of cajoling finally wore Yuri down, though, and he relented, agreeing to travel with Dimitri into the Exclusion Zone.

They decided that they would leave late in the afternoon, take a friend's car to the edge of the forest, then hike the rest of the way in. They would spend the night and following day in the city, then hike out early the next afternoon, returning before they were missed. Dimitri had planned everything out, going so far as to smuggle a Kalash out of his uncle's house a few nights before they left. Both boys had shot the Kalash a few times, but Yuri thought Dimitri was crazy for bringing it.

The most produced rifle in the world, the Avtomat Kalashnikova was as simple as it was elegant. Due to its low manufacturing cost and foolproof design, dozens of imitations of the AK-47 had been made by a variety of countries. There was still some pride in owning one of the original AK's that was produced, though. Designed to be incredibly durable, the Kalash could fire in the heat, cold, rain, mud, sand and just about any other condition on earth.

While most other guns on the battlefield would seize up under bad conditions, the AK-47 thrived in them, requiring virtually no maintenance even after being used and abused. This durability contributed to its popularity, and it quickly became the most illicitly trafficked gun in the entire world. Countries from Albania to China to Venezuela all made their own Kalashnikova variants, some legally and some not. The popularity of the AK-47 was no different in the Ukraine, where many of the ten million firearms in the nation consisted of various AK variants.

"What if the guards catch us with it?" he hissed upon seeing the weapon.

"And what if we run into the wild dogs without it, cousin?"

"That's just another good reason to stay home, Dimitri." Yuri's cousin had simply smiled at this as he wrapped the assault rifle back up in a thick piece of cloth and stashed it under his bed for safekeeping.

Huffing and puffing as he ascended the hill, Yuri had to admit that he was glad they had brought the gun that was currently strapped tight to his cousin's back. Dimitri was very much the soldier, wanting to emulate everything a soldier did, from what they wore to how they walked. Being out on an adventure such as this made this attribute even worse, and Yuri had already forced himself to keep from rolling his eyes at his cousin several times that night.

"There, cousin, do you see?" Dimitri pointed out into the distance, a few miles away, to where the power station was silhouetted against the edge of the rising moon. "We're but an hour away, now!" Yuri hurried down the hill after Dimitri who was practically running at this point, hurrying to reach the city before nightfall.

Chapter Two
Iosif Seleznev | Lucas Pokrov

Iosif and Lucas ran noiselessly down the pavement, scanning to their left and right as they jogged along. Their military boots had received special treatment with a material that reduced their sound in an effort to make them as stealthy as possible. Spread out a few dozen yards from each other, the men breathed heavily as they ran, sweat pouring down their faces. They had been running for over an hour already, and still had another half hour to go before they could stop.

The sun had finally started to set when the helicopter carrying the two Spetsnaz officers had dropped them off near the border of Ukraine and Belarus. Though both officers were Russian, the Ukrainian government had made a special plea for their country's assistance. After a few months of negotiations, the Russian government agreed that it was in the best interest of both countries to send in the covert operatives instead of relying on the local militia, and the top-secret operation began in earnest.

The briefing that Iosif and Lucas received before they left was lacking in detail, as usual, but this particular mission had an air of mysteriousness about it that Lucas was not used to. At 34 years old, Iosif Seleznev was the older of the two officers, with Lucas Pokrov being a mere 27. They had worked together for three years, honing their skills and learning how each other thought so that they could become more effective in combat.

Most of their work had consisted of up front and undercover warfare. Defusing hostage situations, performing anti-terrorism operations, fighting in secret wars overseas and taking on the types of jobs that no other military outfit in their country was capable of handling. This job, however, was different than those.

Your orders are to infiltrate the city of Prip'Yat, which has been emptied of visitors for the next seventy-two hours. You are to cross through the city and the Chernobyl power plant, looking for any signs of strange disturbances roaming the area. Lucas could still hear the briefing they had received, remembering how they had glanced at each other, rolling their eyes at the phrase "strange disturbances." Their orders were clear, though, and they had deployed just two days later, in the midafternoon via a small helicopter that dumped them in a field near the northern road leading into the city.

Once their boots hit the ground, the pair ceased their whispered mocking of the mission description and fell into silence. Regardless of how absurd they thought their mission to be, it was their job to carry out their orders, no matter how they personally felt about them.

When the moon just started to peek over the horizon, the two men stopped, kneeling on the pavement as they reviewed their GPS trackers and radiation detectors.

"Rads in the green." Lucas scanned the ground and the surrounding air with the radiation detector.

"We're on course," Iosif whispered back. "Switch to your filters once we hit the grass."

Lucas nodded and unconsciously felt his chest to make sure his face mask filter was still in place. Though the dangers of radiation in Prip'Yat were somewhat exaggerated, there were still hot patches of radiation where you could get a potentially lethal dose if you stood still for too long. Along with moving quickly through foliage, the two would wear their face masks at all times to keep from inhaling radioactive particles.

Iosif slid the GPS unit back into a pouch on his vest and motioned for them to continue forward. Lucas waited until Iosif was several paces ahead before he stood up and began jogging along as well. They were within sight of the bridge on the north end of the city. Once the bridge was crossed, they would go into full tactical mode, shouldering their weapons and preparing to combat any threats they faced.

Chapter Three
Yuri Volkov | Dimitri Alexeiev

The silence of the city of Prip'Yat was unique and deafening, a constant reminder of the emptiness of the area. Once a bustling metropolis, home to fifty thousand residents, it was but a ghost town now, one of the only true ghost towns still left in the world. Completely abandoned with naught but a few hours' notice, the residents of the city had only enough time to carry themselves out during the evacuation. There was no time to grab anything beyond a few personal possessions, but most of the residents – believing they would only be evacuated for a few days – didn't even take those. Apartment buildings that once held thousands of people were now empty, towering into the sky, their windows and doors broken from the vandals and looters who were foolish enough to enter the city.

Although there were still pockets of high-level radiation, the more insidious danger came from a slightly different avenue. Tiny radioactive particles still clung to every surface of the buildings and the ground in and around the city. Brushing up against the particles would contaminate your skin and clothing, which merely meant that you had to dispose of your clothing and scrub yourself before returning to your home.

The worse threat from the particles was getting them inside your body where they wouldn't have to contend with going through layers of cloth and skin before reaching vital organs. Inhaling or eating radioactive particles could be devastating to your body, depending on the quantity consumed. For the residents and tourists of Kiev, dealing with radiation had become a normal part of life, and their guard sometimes dropped. Someone would walk through the Exclusion Zone and not wash their hands before eating. Someone would go through a building and not rinse their shoes off before reentering their vehicle. Little things like this contributed to the slow relaxing of safety precautions by those who visited the Zone, despite the best warnings from the Ukrainian government and the more cautious individuals.

Though aware of the dangers of radiation, Dimitri and Yuri were two victims of this growing laxness about safety precautions. They walked directly through tall grasses in the fields around Prip'Yat, brushing it with their hands and then touching their faces as they adjusted their balaclavas. Though the radiation was invisible, odorless and tasteless, it was still present.

"Are you sure this is the right way, Dimitri?" The pair had been walking for nearly an hour, watching as the twilight gave way to the darkness that enveloped them in the landscape, rendering them nearly invisible in their dark clothing.

"Yes, cousin, for the hundredth time, I'm sure! We are almost there, just on the other side of these trees."

Once they were clear of the checkpoints and well into the Exclusion Zone, Dimitri pulled out a map that was printed on several pieces of paper held together with paperclips. He studied it under his flashlight as they walked, trying to find landmarks in the darkness. He was as sure as he could be that they were on the right path, but he was starting to wonder himself if they had taken the wrong route and walked past the city altogether.

"There, up ahead!" Yuri tapped Dimitri on the shoulder, pointing in front of them.

Through the trees, dark square shadows rose up, solidifying into buildings, windows and doorways. The cousins walked in silence out of the forest, standing before an enormous apartment building. The paint on the outside had long since cracked and faded, scattered to the winds by time and nature. Balconies stood out on each floor of the apartment building even in the dim light of the dusk, offset by rows upon rows of matching windows, two per apartment. The cousins walked around the building, giving it a wide berth as they stared up at it towering over them.

Around the apartment, more buildings stretched up, rising into view as they contrasted with the rising moon. Ahead through the maze of apartments stretched a long clear path, the main road into and out of Prip'Yat. Here in the heart of the city there were no guardhouses and no residents, only animals, trees and grass. Dimitri and Yuri walked in silence and awe of the city that surrounded them, taken aback by the serenity. Miles away, back in their homes, the sound of traffic was a constant and ever-present background noise. Here, though, the only sound was an occasional insect, chirping or buzzing in the distance.

The cousins walked on to the main road, standing on the blacktop. They pulled off their balaclavas, turning around in wonder, shining their flashlights up at the buildings that surrounded them.

Dimitri grinned at his younger companion. "Welcome to Prip'Yat, cousin."

Chapter Four
Iosif Seleznev | Lucas Pokrov

Trained as a sniper, Lucas trailed behind Iosif by several yards, scanning the rooftops and thick vegetation for any signs of movement. His thick mask made breathing more difficult, and both men wheezed as they struggled to take in enough oxygen through the thick filters. Iosif kept his assault rifle pressed firmly against his shoulder as he walked down the side of the road, using the infrared scope to look for any signs of movement in the area. Behind him, Lucas used a thermal scope on his SVD to check for heat signatures. For the moment, the city was quiet and devoid of movement, but the men stayed alert as they moved.

Though he was only twenty-seven years old, Lucas felt like he was sixty. Years of back-to-back missions – both inside Russia and into foreign territories – had quickly eaten away at his youthful demeanor. An orphan with no siblings or relatives to care for him, Lucas grew up in an underfunded and overcrowded Children's Home in Moscow. Once he reached the age of eighteen, he joined the military and quickly rose through the ranks. Lucas had an unwavering commitment to his new way of life and though his rebellious nature had been repressed by his training, it was still there, lurking underneath the surface. He followed all orders he was given without question, though he did often ponder the operations he was tasked with carrying out, wondering how much of the truth he was being told.

Lucas thought back to one of the briefings they had undergone in preparation for the mission as he walked. *Do not rely solely on your equipment or on your eyes. You must split your attention between the two. The disturbance you are investigating does not always show up on thermal or infrared, and we have had reports of it vanishing from plain sight.* Based on the ludicrous mission briefing, Lucas was certain that they would turn up empty handed, and that the true purpose of the mission was to satisfy some bored bureaucrat sitting behind a mahogany desk.

Assholes, sending us out on a wild good chase like this. Lucas snorted in derision, prompting a quick look back from his superior. Lucas nodded curtly in response to the look he received and pushed the negative thoughts of the mission from his mind. A few days spent in a place where they were certain to not get shot at sounded almost like a vacation, despite the mask and the weight of their equipment.

According to their maps and GPS, Iosif and Lucas were passing through a wooded area near the stadium in Prip'Yat, at the northeastern end of the town. The road branched off into a few different directions, but the two soldiers moved through the trees and brush, preferring the cover of the vegetation to the openness of the road.

On their left was a vast area of sand and dirt, completely devoid of trees, bushes and all but the hardiest of grasses. This area had been a dumping ground for radioactive sand from the waters around the city, and concrete barriers were set up to prevent the contaminated sand and soil from washing into the nearby river. Lucas glanced down at his radiation meter, which had spiked briefly but was back down at a reasonable level. As the two didn't venture onto the sand itself, they would be safe from the majority of the radiation in the area.

After a few minutes of hurried walking, Lucas glanced to the west and saw the silhouette of chairs that marked the nearby stadium. He tapped the button for the secure communications link between himself and Iosif and spoke softly.

"We're passing the stadium. Any signs of movement?"

Ahead of him, in the dark, Iosif stopped and knelt down in a patch of dirt as he responded. "A few animals, nothing more. Definitely no 'monster' or whatever the hell we're looking for. Let's stop for a moment."

Lucas confirmed the decision and stood still, not wanting to touch any more of the grass around them than he had to.

After half a minute had passed, Lucas flexed his arms, ready to get moving gain. "Where to now?"

Iosif scanned the area ahead of them with his rifle and pointed forward along the bank of the lake that was near the radioactive sand. "Let's move up to the hospital. That's one of the scan locations marked on our checklist."

Iosif stood and moved forward again, with Lucas behind him. As the moon continued to rise in the sky, a few clouds began to drift toward them, gradually starting to block out the ambient light and forcing the pair to rely more heavily on their thermal and infrared sights in the darkness. As the shadows of the clouds moved along the ground from the west to the east, off in the distance, too far away for them to notice, a shadow moved perpendicular to those from the clouds as it wound its way through the city.

Chapter Five
Yuri Volkov | Dimitri Alexeiev

While planning their trip, Dimitri and Yuri had carefully checked the tour guide schedules, finding – to their amazement – that none had been scheduled by any tour agency for a three day period. This was very rare, and Dimitri had been overjoyed to see that it coincided with the annual school camping trip. Dimitri was ruthless in his insisting that they go. "It's a sign from God that we should explore!" Yuri was less convinced of this fact, but eventually relented to Dimitri.

Despite the promise of no scheduled tours, there was always the possibility of running into an impromptu exploration like their own, or encountering an extremely rare guard patrol through the area. The larger threat, though, came from the animals that called the city home. Though they stayed in the wilderness areas during the day, they would occasionally venture into the city at night to scavenge for food. Wild dogs, interbred for generations, were the biggest danger since they traveled in packs and had virtually no fear of humans. Bears were less common, though every once in a while a tour group would have a close encounter with one in the city during the early morning or late evening.

"We'll explore the city tonight and tomorrow morning, Yuri. It'll be glorious!" Dimitri and Yuri were still taken aback by the sight of the city and the fact that they were finally standing in its center, a place they had imagined for years but never had the opportunity to see in person until now. The chill of the night air grew in intensity, making both cousins glad for the large down jackets that they were both wearing. Dimitri still held on to his Kalash, though it was loosened now, shaking back and forth on his back as he walked.

Prip'Yat was a city reclaimed by nature and undergoing a reverse transformation. Once a city of steel and cement, it was returning to a natural state. Grass, weeds and bushes cracked the streets and sidewalks, trees grew in the center of abandoned fountains and vines covered entire buildings, slowly cracking away at their shells. In another fifty years, the city would be unrecognizable, completely consumed by the world around it.

The encroachment of nature upon the city meant that radiation hotspots were more frequent and better hidden, disguised in clumps of trees or in the tall grass. Without a Geiger counter, the cousins moved quickly, sticking to the main roads and sidewalks while avoiding the open areas around the city. The roads, while still contaminated, offered better protection than the surrounding grass, and less of a chance of happening upon a hotspot. Yuri kept an eye on his disposable radiation meter. It had climbed by a few ticks since he last checked, but the movement was slow and his total exposure was still well within the safe zone.

Massive trees grew in the city square, their thick foliage rustling quietly in the breeze. Dimitri and Yuri's boots ticked softly on the pavement as they walked, making a beeline for the Palace of Culture on the northwest side of the square. A common theme in the Soviet era, Palaces of Culture typically contained movie theaters, swimming pools and studios where the inhabitants of a city could meet and interact. Prip'Yat was no exception, though the once beautiful building was torn apart – glass, wood and metal littering the floors.

The crack of debris under the feet of the cousins was unnerving in the silence as they climbed the steps, entering the main section of the Palace of Culture. The Ferris wheel was visible out the front of the Palace. As one of the most iconic images representing the Chernobyl disaster and the city of Prip'Yat, the Ferris wheel was also one of the most dangerous, harboring extreme amounts of radiation. While it was a potentially lethal place to visit, it nonetheless remained a tantalizing target.

Stairs wound upwards into the large building and corridors snaked off in every direction, with new discoveries waiting to be uncovered. The twin flashlight beams from Yuri and Dimitri cut through the shadows of the building as they turned around, staring at the arched ceiling, then looked at each other.

Dimitri spoke with a grin. "Where first, cousin?"

Chapter Six
Iosif Seleznev | Lucas Pokrov

Iosif held a closed fist up, signaling for Lucas to stop. Lucas crouched low to the ground, sweeping his SVD to the left, right and back of the pair for any signs of trouble. A click came through on his earpiece followed by Iosif's voice.

"Moving past the hospital now. Go slow, check the roofs, I'll take the ground."

Lucas tapped the microphone button once to signify an affirmative response. Following Iosif's lead, he began to circle the hospital, giving it a wide berth and keeping several yards between him and his comrade.

From one hundred yards away, the soldiers could see nearly every section of the hospital at once, a fact that Lucas used to his full advantage. After doing a scan of the roof of the hospital with his thermal scope, he began to scan the long rows of windows, looking for any unusual heat signatures. The side of the building was dark blue in the cold of the night and the windows were black with no other colors to be seen.

After moving several paces forward, Lucas flipped his thermal scope down to the right on the SVD and flipped up a second scope that had been locked into place on the opposite side of the rifle. This scope was of lesser magnification and allowed him to see in infrared. After a quick check through the infrared scope, he tapped the microphone button and spoke.

"Nothing on either band. Doing a visual scan, then circling around the rear." A single click in his earpiece told him that Iosif had received his message and wanted him to proceed.

Lucas pulled a small pair of binoculars out of a pouch on his vest and scanned the building one final time, checking to see if anything was visible. *What's going to show up that wasn't on either scope, though?* Orders were orders, though, and Lucas obeyed them to the letter.

Satisfied that nothing was in the windows or on the roof of the hospital on the eastern side, Lucas began to circle around the northern part of the building, moving to check the western side of the hospital and then link up with Iosif at the entrance on the south side of the structure.

Without the thermal or infrared scopes, the hospital was both dark and uninviting. The exterior façade was damaged and crumbling, and the tan paint was barely visible in the moonlight. Craggy trees devoid of leaves had grown close around the building in the last few decades and their haphazard shadows were cast over the ground and the building, shaking as the trees vibrated in the breeze.

A senior ranking officer for two years, Iosif Seleznev was no stranger to hostile environments, though he grudgingly admitted to himself that this city was the first in a long time to evoke any type of emotion in him. Wading through swamps, crawling through deserts and being outnumbered by enemies ten-to-one didn't rattle him. This city spooked him, though. Iosif couldn't pinpoint what exactly had put him on edge, but he trusted his gut, so he stayed alert as he cautiously approached the hospital.

On the opposite side of the hospital from Iosif, Lucas was finishing his thermal and infrared sweeps of the windows and roof of the building. After lowering his rifle, he turned to the side to readjust his face mask before conducting a final visual sweep. The mask was stifling even in the cold air, and he dearly wished he could remove it. His Geiger counter still showed slightly high radiation levels, though, so he kept the mask on, not wanting to have to be subjected to the intensive radiation poisoning treatment that was mandatory for soldiers when they returned from missions. Radiation contamination up to a certain level was tolerated, but anything beyond that got you a week in isolation, drinking gallons of chemicals designed to flush the radiation from your body. In Lucas's mind, a few days with a mask was preferable to that type of experience.

Lucas turned back to check the hospital building one last time with his binoculars when movement at the edge of his field of view caught his eye. He whipped his head toward the movement, bringing his scope up to scan for it. The infrared scope was still in place and he squinted through it, trying to find the source of the movement again. Fifteen hundred yards away, in between several apartment buildings and countless trees, Lucas made out the faintest flicker of movement, a dark shadow darting behind the buildings. Adrenaline pumped through his body as he pushed his microphone button and spoke quickly to Iosif.

"Movement west, through the buildings, half a kilometer out. Looked like a big shadow moving fast."

Iosif's voice was hurried as he replied. "Move out. I'll pick up and follow behind you."

Lucas was already up and running before Iosif finished his reply. As he ran, he jabbed the microphone button once and then broke into a sprint, dodging low hanging branches and running around rubble, trees and bushes that grew throughout the city, heading in the direction of the shadow.

Chapter Seven
Yuri Volkov | Dimitri Alexeiev

Walking along the main road, Dimitri and Yuri were quiet, soaking in the ambience of the city as they took in the sights. After leaving the Palace of Culture, they kept their lights off as they walked south, admiring the apartments and wide open spaces that surrounded them. Wandering aimlessly along, the cousins had no real plans of where to go next, so they continued to go from building to building, slowly winding their way around and through the area.

The interior of the apartment buildings were both surprising and intimidating to the cousins. Filled with trash and remnants of personal effects, nearly every room had been picked over by looters and vandals a dozen or more times. Thick layers of dust and dirt coated the floors, blown in by the wind through the broken windows. Footprints were scattered across the floor as well, and if you looked closely enough, you could discern how long ago they were made by how much they had been filled in by dirt and debris.

Dimitri and Yuri moved quickly through the apartments, not wanting to linger for too long in the dust they were stirring up for fear that it could be contaminated with radiation. They stuck to the ground and second stories of the buildings, being mindful of the condition of the floors which were sagging and rotting from years of water damage. The wood and laminate were broken clean through in more than a few spots, signs that someone had become an inadvertent victim of a poorly timed misstep.

As the pair walked through a hallway of one of the westernmost apartments, Yuri tugged on Dimitri's shirt and motioned for him to stop. The darkness of the apartments had forced the boys to turn on their flashlights. They kept their hands pressed against the front of the lights, though, allowing only the smallest sliver of a beam to shine through the cracks in their fingers. In the luminescence of his flashlight, Yuri had caught sight of something shining on the floor and stopped, getting Dimitri to stop as well.

"What the hell?" Dimitri murmured as he knelt down next to Yuri, who was already squatting in front of the object on the floor.

"It looks like... piss?" Yuri looked up at his older cousin, then back down at the floor. He moved his hand to the side of his flashlight and kept the beam tight on the floor, fully illuminating the object. Under the light, the object shimmered as Yuri passed the flashlight back and forth over its surface. Unlike urine, the object on the floor was not flat, but looked more like a pile of gel, nearly crystal clear with the faintest hint of grey and yellow in it. Dimitri leaned in closer and sniffed deeply, then grimaced and backed up.

"It smells like petroleum. Maybe it's a leak from something, or a tourist dropped it."

Yuri shook his head slowly. "No, it couldn't be."

Dimitri looked up from the pile of goop on the floor, staring at Yuri questioningly. Yuri swallowed hard as he looked at the floor, shining his light back and forth. "No footprints. We're the only ones who've been in here in a long time. This looks fresh."

Dimitri felt a chill run up his spine as Yuri spoke. He stood up suddenly, shaking his arms and head as he tried to ignore the fear that was threatening to take hold. "Whatever it is, let's just leave it alone and get out of here."

Yuri nodded slowly and stood up to follow Dimitri, who was already halfway down the hall, heading for the doorway. Yuri backed slowly down the hall, keeping his light trained on the object, half expecting it to start moving when he wasn't watching. Yuri finally switched his light off at the main door to the apartments and shuffled out the door, following Dimitri. The pair walked swiftly away from the apartments, heading back up the main road toward the square and the Palace of Culture.

After only a few paces, Dimitri felt another chill and he slowed down to allow Yuri to catch up, whispering to him as they strolled along.

"Something doesn't feel right here. It's like we're being watched."

Yuri felt his stomach turn at Dimitri's words, distraught at hearing his cousin confirm the very thing he had feared ever since they first saw the object on the floor. As the two quickened their pace, a crackle sounded in the distance, along with a rustling in the trees. Both boys broke into a run without thinking about it, heading into the main square and dashing into the nearest building they could find. In a full blown panic, neither Yuri nor Dimitri had the presence of mind to pay attention to where they were going as they charged headlong down a flight of stairs into a darkened corridor.

Chapter Eight
Iosif Seleznev | Lucas Pokrov

Running alone through thick vegetation while simultaneously trying to pay attention to one's surroundings in a dark environment was difficult enough. Doing so while in pursuit of a fleeting movement in the distance that could very well have just been the shadow from a cloud added an extra layer of complexity to the situation. Lucas stayed focused as he ran, regulating his breathing through the face mask and stopping every few seconds to scan the area ahead with his scope. Behind him, Iosif brought up the rear, performing the same series of actions as he ran to catch up.

With the hospital left unexplored, the soldiers still considered it a potential danger zone, and both of them periodically checked behind them as they ran forward, quickly closing the half kilometer distance to their target location. Lucas's breathing was loud in his ear, a symptom of the full face mask that covered the front half of his head, including his ears. As a single piece of polymer-matrix composite, the mask didn't restrict the user's view at all, which was a far cry from the older protective gear that soldiers used to wear.

Although the face filter was bulky and made it difficult to breathe, the mask did offer one additional advantage. Due to its construction, it was able to withstand severe blows, including rounds up into a 9mm caliber. Larger rounds would penetrate the mask, but their penetration power was vastly reduced, meaning that even if you were shot in the face, you had a much higher chance of surviving than if you weren't wearing it.

Slight negative pressure generated by a small pump on the mask ensured that it always had an airtight seal over the wearer's face, which was reinforced by the pair of heavy-duty rubber straps that encircled Iosif's and Lucas's heads. In addition to providing impact protection and keeping the wearer safe from radiation, the masks also filtered out chemical and biological contaminants. Though the pair didn't expect to need their masks for those particular use cases, they both had enough experience dealing with the unknown to appreciate the protection even if it wasn't absolutely essential.

Passing through a thicket of trees, Lucas slowed as he neared the spot where he had caught the movement. He scanned the ground and the surrounding buildings, road, and vegetation with his rifle scope, but nothing was visible.

Iosif had finally caught up next to him and crouched nearby, breathing heavily as he spoke.

"What did you see?"

Lucas continued to scan the area as he replied, switching between his thermal and infrared scopes. "Not sure. It was big, though, and moving fast. It disappeared here, between the buildings."

"Did it show up on the scopes?"

"Negative. I had finished a scan when I saw it whip past and I took off after it."

Iosif held his radiation meter aloft, waving it around them to scan the air and the ground. "Radiation levels seem normal here. Got anything on the thermal?"

Lucas's thermal scanner on his scope was sensitive enough that it could pick up trace amounts of heat left in the footprints of animals for a few moments after they had passed. He had checked the ground several times since stopping, though, and had found no evidence of any residual heat.

"Nothing."

Iosif sighed and looked around, getting his bearings. "This is the first sign of anything we've had tonight, so let's stay on top of it. It was heading north, right?"

Lucas nodded. "Affirmative. Rapidly, too."

"Okay, let's head to the next checkpoint since it's north of here. We'll hit the hospital on our way out."

Iosif ran past Lucas, breaking from cover on the east side of the main road and moving to the west side. Lucas continued striding up on the east side of the road, keeping close to the buildings as he moved. He trailed behind Iosif's position by several yards as before, maintaining a close eye on the rooftops of the buildings as they moved past, alert for any signs of movement.

The road was empty and devoid of heat signatures or movement, though Lucas couldn't deny feeling nervous as they worked their way north into the city. In past missions, when they had been alone in the darkness, they had always known who their enemy was and that he was out there somewhere, hiding in the dark. Pursuing an unknown enemy in a territory that was completely devoid of life was a new experience, one that Lucas didn't appreciate.

Chapter Nine
Yuri Volkov | Dimitri Alexeiev

Once Dimitri and Yuri finally stopped running, Yuri had to brace himself against the wall to keep from toppling over. His heart was beating hard in his chest, feeling like it was about to burst from pumping so much blood, making him light-headed and dizzy. Dimitri held onto Yuri with one arm, pushing his other arm against his side as he arched his back and looked at the ceiling, panting with exhaustion.

"You know," Dimitri finally wheezed, "We're just a couple of babies. That was nothing but animal shit and the wind!" Yuri glanced up at Dimitri, seeing the hesitation in his cousin's eyes as he spoke. Dimitri didn't believe what he said and neither did Yuri, but Yuri felt obligated to agree with his cousin, if only to try and bring calm to the situation.

He nodded slowly as he regained control of his breathing. "Yeah, that's all it was." Yuri's voice was shaking, but he put on a brave smile, trying to make the best of the situation. "At least we didn't meet the bear that left it, right?"

Dimitri's grin was genuine as he laughed at Yuri, punching him lightly in the shoulder.

"Come on, let's stop being such children." He shined his flashlight around the room they were in, trying to figure out what building they had run into. "Might as well explore this place, whatever it is."

Yuri flicked on his light as well and moved it slowly over the interior walls and columns, squinting through the dust and reflections from the light. "It's big. Maybe a market?"

Dimitri shook his head. "We came down two flights of stairs, remember? I don't think a market would have that many steps."

Yuri waved a hand in front of his face, shooing away the dust motes that swirled as he walked through the cavernous room. The walls were a pale pink in color, though the paint was cracked and fading. Thick pillars were covered in elaborate and colorful paintings, remnants of the decorations that once adorned the walls. Small wheelchairs and beds were overturned in the basement, lending a sad tone to the room. As Yuri's flashlight beam passed over these items, he suddenly realized where they were. *This must be the children's clinic,* he thought.

As the only children's hospital in the area, any child with an injury would have been sent here instead of to the main hospital, staying for as little as a few hours or as long as a few months. When the disaster occurred, though, all of the children in the clinic had to be immediately evacuated despite their various ailments and conditions. While there was no proof, Dimitri and Yuri had often spoken of the children who might have died during the evacuation, either too wounded to survive the trip out of the city or simply forgotten. The thought of being in a building that may have contained those exact children was enough to spook the both of them more than the strange puddle in the apartment building, though they each tried their best not to show their apprehension.

Yuri looked back at the footprints his boots left in the dust, doing his best to breathe shallowly, not wanting to inhale any more radiation than he already was. "Come on, cousin. Let's get out of here. We should find someplace a little less ominous to explore."

Dimitri grunted in response, crouching over a broken picture frame on the floor. A small child in a dress who was carrying a flower in her hands was faded and torn under the broken glass. Dimitri found himself lost in the photograph, wondering who the little girl was and what her life was like before the disaster.

"Those poor souls." Dimitri mumbled, momentarily forgetting his adventurer spirit. Yuri pressed a hand on Dimitri's shoulder, making him jump in surprise.

"Yes, sorry. You're right. Let's go. This place is far too disturbing to stay in for long."

"What about the noise we heard?" Yuri motioned upwards, referring to the cracks and rustles they had heard earlier.

"Just the wind, remember?" Dimitri smiled, trying his best to appear brave to his cousin.

Yuri began to nod in agreement when a noise from the upstairs level of the clinic stopped both cousins in their tracks. The noise was quiet at first, like the light scraping of two pieces of wood against each other. It came in spurts, stopping for several seconds, starting up and then stopping again.

"That is *not* the wind." Yuri leaned in to Dimitri's ear and hissed at him as quietly as he could manage.

Although Yuri was quiet when he spoke, the sounds from upstairs changed the very second the words left his mouth. The slow scraping became louder and more frenzied, and was accompanied by more sounds of crackling, like a combination between leaves crunching and the arc of electricity. The sound continued to circle above the boys as they stood frozen in fear, Yuri still holding onto Dimitri's coat.

Dimitri looked at Yuri in panic as the sound began to change. Instead of staying in one location as it had, it began to move outward, sounding as though its source could be moving closer to the stairwell that led to the basement. The pair waved their flashlights about the room wildly, striving to be quiet at the same time as they searched for an exit from the building.

Yuri pointed out into the hall and motioned for Dimitri to follow him. The room they were in had no other way out, and Yuri didn't want to get trapped in the room if the source of the sounds upstairs decided to join them in the basement. Although the boys stepped lightly through the room, they could hear the noise from upstairs growingly increasingly agitated. When they reached the door, though, all hell broke loose.

Dimitri's shoulder brushed the door to the room they were in as they exited, causing its hinges to give off a loud squeal. Instantly the noise from upstairs changed from a soft scratching to a harried scrabbling combined with the sounds of thumping. Yuri shoved Dimitri forward, nearly knocking him down. "Get moving now!" Yuri hissed again at Dimitri, glancing behind him at the stairs they had descended a short time ago.

Dimitri held his light in front of him as he ran, trying to find another stairwell or other avenue of escape. The noise from upstairs began to recede behind them as they ran away from the stairs, then it grew stronger and louder. Panicked, the cousins turned a blind corner in the hallway, realizing that whatever was making the sound was now down in the basement and likely hot in pursuit of them.

At the end of the hall, Yuri spotted an object that made his heart leap. A janitorial closet was positioned in the hallway, with its door wide open. Just inside the closet the beams of their flashlights reflected off a piece of glass high on the far wall of the closet.

"Window!" Yuri half shouted at Dimitri as they ran, struggling to stay ahead of the thing behind them. Dimitri was first in the closet, followed close by Yuri who slammed the door to the closet shut, wincing as it bounced back open, the handle and lock having broken off long ago.

"Hurry up!" Yuri shone his light out of the janitorial closet and back down the long hall. A dark shape charged along, running past the branch that the boys had taken. Behind him, Dimitri had finally gotten the window open and shouldered boxes in front of it, building a makeshift staircase to get up to the window.

"Okay, let's go!" Dimitri shouted down at Yuri from the top of the boxes, his body already halfway out the window.

Yuri grabbed Dimitri's outstretched hand and began to descend the stairway of boxes. He couldn't resist one last look behind him as he climbed, and directed his light back down the hallway. The dark shape reappeared at the end of the hall, half hidden by the partially closed janitorial close door. It was a large, black shape, as wide as it was tall, with no definable form. Although the thing was just as dark as the basement they were in, Yuri could sense its shape, feeling adrenaline coarse through his veins as fear gripped his heart.

Spurred on by the sight, Yuri squirmed through the window, digging his fingers into the dirt and grass that were just outside. Dimitri grabbed Yuri's arm and hauled him up. The boys stumbled as they began to run, trying to get as far away from the clinic as possible.

Chapter Ten
Iosif Seleznev | Lucas Pokrov

When Lucas's boot first made a squishing sound, he didn't think much of it. Only after he had trouble moving his foot did he look down to see what was keeping it in place. In the darkness, he had trouble making it out, so he pulled out a small flashlight from his vest pocket and turned on the red filter, shining a pale red light down on the ground.

The red light reflected and shimmered off the surface of the substance that surrounded his boot. It was only a few inches high, but it was like glue and kept his foot still, preventing him from moving.

"What the hell..." Lucas mumbled to himself, then he keyed his microphone.

"I've got something back here."

Up ahead, Iosif stopped and turned around. Lucas waved him back, then crouched down, looking around to make sure that he was safe as he examined the substance around his boot.

"Report." Iosif stood just a few feet away, scanning the area around them.

"Something's got my boot. I can barely budge it."

Iosif pointed his rifle down at Lucas's boot, viewing it through his infrared scope. He bent down, examining the substance under the red light, then pulled out a knife from his belt.

"Hold still." Iosif stuck the knife into the substance, which showed no reaction as he cut through it. The knife passed through cleanly, making a clear incision around the edge of Lucas's boot as Iosif cut him loose. Once he finished cutting, he pulled the knife out of the substance and stood up.

"Okay, pull hard, quickly."

Lucas braced himself on his left leg and jerked his right leg back and up. With a loud snap, his boot came free and he started to tumble backward. Iosif reached out and grabbed his arm, keeping him from falling.

"What the hell is that?" Lucas shook his boot as he spoke, trying to remove the remnants of the substance from it without success. Iosif was once again on a knee, examining the substance up close, lost in thought.

"Shit, not this stuff again." Iosif spoke to himself, not keying the microphone, though the soldiers were close enough to each other that Lucas could still make out what he said through their masks.

"What do you mean? This isn't like anything I've seen before." Lucas leaned down to get a closer look. While the substance had sounded like a liquid or gel when he stepped in it, Lucas could see that it was now completely solid. The substance was opaque in color, with a slight white and grey tint to it.

Iosif looked up at Lucas, meeting his gaze for a moment without speaking. He reached into his vest pocket, pulled out a small object and then pressed it into Lucas's hand.

"I need you to hold on to this for me. I'll take it back once we finish our sweep."

Lucas looked down at the small notebook in his hand in confusion. He started to open it when Iosif shook his head. "No. Just keep it in your pocket for me."

Lucas nodded slowly and stuffed the notebook into the front of his vest, unsure what to make of his partner's behavior. Iosif stood and continued moving down the road, scanning the area as he had before. "Stay alert. It looks like this wild goose chase is turning into a real hunt."

Lucas moved forward, hanging behind Iosif as they advanced through the city as he tried to put the notebook out of his mind. "Sir, what were you talking about with that stuff?"

Iosif kept moving, not replying for a moment. Finally, Lucas heard the hiss of an open communication line. Iosif had depressed the button for his microphone, but was hesitating to speak. "I can't say anything about it, I'm sorry. I want to, but I can't."

Operational security was crucial for soldiers and Lucas understood this well. Although he was technically the same rank as Iosif, he still fell into the habit of calling him "sir" and looking up to him as his superior. If Iosif knew anything, Lucas trusted him enough to speak up if it was serious. Until then, he decided, he'd just keep his mouth shut about it and try to push the questions from his mind.

After several moments of walking in silence, Iosif spoke again. "I've got another one here."

Lucas pulled up his scope and zeroed in on Iosif's location ahead of him. Enlarged in the scope, the object was difficult to make out at first, though it quickly became apparent that it was the same substance that Lucas had become trapped in earlier. Lucas moved up next to Iosif who had crouched down next to the substance, viewing it from mere inches away.

"Don't touch it. Just watch." Iosif motioned for Lucas to stand back, then pulled out his knife again. The knife blade was clean, unlike Lucas's boot, which still had remnants of the hard substance on it. Iosif slid the knife into the substance quickly, slicing it from side to side. The substance quivered like gelatin as the knife moved through it, and Lucas could hear the same squishing sound he'd heard when he'd stepped in it earlier.

Within seconds the substance started to change. The color darkened, going from clear to opaque. The consistency changed as well and it turned from being soft and malleable to hard and rock-like, freezing the knife in place and holding it firmly upright. Iosif let go of the knife and shook his head, watching the substance finish its rapid transformation.

Lucas said nothing as he watched, and he kept checking the area around them for signs of trouble. With a grunt, Iosif grabbed the knife and pulled hard on it, flexing it from side to side. The blade finally came loose and Iosif held out his hand to Lucas. "Give me your knife."

Lucas pulled out his knife and handed it to Iosif, who used it to scrape dried chunks of the strange substance off of his own knife. Once his blade was clean again, he passed back Lucas's knife and they both sheathed their blades. Iosif gave Lucas a look before turning around and continuing down the road. Once again Lucas was overwhelmed with questions, but Iosif's look was enough to keep him quiet. *Later. I can find out later.*

As the pair moved forward, Lucas was grateful that they didn't run into any more patches of the strange material either on or off the road. This gratitude was tempered by the new phenomenon that reared its head once the pair entered the main square of the city.

With several large buildings and a tall, decorative arch surrounding the city square, it was the official hub of the city of Prip'Yat before the disaster. It was also one of the loudest parts of the city, with sounds easily reflecting off the long patches of pavement and the walls of the surrounding buildings. On a quiet night the square would be relatively peaceful, though that was not the case on this night.

A soft scraping echoed out across the square, barely audible to the soldiers. Microphones implanted in their masks picked up and amplified external sounds, though even with this advantage it still took a few seconds for Iosif and Lucas to realize that a sound was even present. Iosif noticed the sound first and immediately threw himself to the ground, bringing the scope of his rifle up to his eye as he scanned the area in front of them.

Upon seeing Iosif dive to the ground, Lucas moved back into the shadow of some nearby trees, unsure of what was going on but reacting with swiftness to his partner's movements. He whispered as he tapped the microphone button. "What do you have?"

"Shut up and listen!" Iosif whispered back angrily, causing Lucas to grow quiet and hold his breath. He, too, began to hear the noise echoing around them. It was strange and out of place, and Lucas couldn't think of what might be causing it. He popped up his thermal and night vision scopes, but didn't see anything out of the ordinary in their immediate vicinity. Lucas was just about to key his microphone when Iosif charged forward, speaking to him at the same time.

"It's got to be in there! Move!"

Lucas waited until Iosif was in the middle of the square before following him in. The two men raced up a set of stairs into a squat building, with Lucas trailing behind to provide cover from the rear. Iosif slowed his ascent as he moved through the door of the building, keeping his rifle scope to one eye to take advantage of the infrared sight. Both soldiers shuffled into the building, entering a large foyer with a greeting desk and the remnants of dozens of chairs scattered about. Iosif pointed to the left side of the desk, motioning for Lucas to move in that direction. The pair kept to opposite sides of the building, stepping around slowly and deliberately while they breathed as softly as possible, trying to pick up on any trace of the noise they heard outside.

Chapter Eleven
Yuri Volkov | Dimitri Alexeiev

Dimitri and Yuri were both more frightened than they had been before in their lives. Fearful glances back at the building as they stumbled along didn't reveal any pursuers, though they weren't about to take any chances by slowing down. Trees whipped by, slapping them in the face as they raced through a wooded area, running directly away from the children's clinic. Out of nowhere, the trees ended and the road began, along with the introduction of more moonlight that was no longer blocked by the woods.

Yuri nearly tripped as they ran into the road, catching his foot on the edge of the pavement as he jumped a few inches. Dimitri wasn't so lucky, though, and caught his toes on the cement. He slammed into the ground, rolling as he went. The sleeve of his jacket was jerked up his arm by the friction of the road surface, scraping his bare arm on the pavement as his leftover momentum propelled him forward.

Yuri hurried back to Dimitri and helped him up and they took off again. Dimitri held his injured arm as he ran, fighting to keep his Kalash on his shoulder. He didn't feel any major pain from the fall aside from the long scrapes on his arm and the flow of adrenaline kept him from noticing more than a slight twinge from that.

The cousins stayed on the road as they ran, still heading away from the clinic. It was a major road with buildings alongside it. Apartments were on the right while a market and other consumer shops were on the left, marked by their tall glassless windows. These stores, similar to the others scattered around the city, were once full of pharmaceuticals, groceries, and household goods that were sold to the residents of the city. None of the windows remained in the stores, though the remnants of scattered shopping carts spoke to the once bustling area.

After several minutes of silent running, Dimitri began to slow down, prompting Yuri to slow as well. "What's the matter?" Yuri whispered to his cousin, still fearful of whatever might be behind them.

Dimitri said nothing as he raised his injured arm, pointing ahead down the road. A small field lay at the end of the paved road, with a dirt path leading from the road to a structure just beyond the field. Though it was difficult to make out in the darkness, as the cousins crossed through the field it quickly became apparent that the structure was a greenhouse.

Like the windows on the shops and other buildings in the city, the glass on the greenhouse had suffered the same fate. Large and small pieces lay scattered inside and outside the steel structure which was itself covered in vines and creeping plants that had overtaken it. Most of the equipment from inside the greenhouse had been stolen or damaged by vandals, but a few rows of planting containers still remained as a confirmation of what the building had been used for.

Working with a catalyst like the greenhouse, nature had moved more swiftly in this area than it had in the rest of the city. Nearly three hundred yards long by seventy-five yards wide, it was a massive structure, though all that was left of it was the metal frame. Spray paint adorned the metal poles of the greenhouse, giving evidence of the vandals that had been through countless times.

Dimitri pushed aside a tree branch as he stopped low under a fallen metal support, holding the branch up for Yuri to follow. The cracking of the glass underfoot was quieter here, muffled by the trees and grass growing in and around the structure. While you once may have been able to see from one end of the greenhouse to the other, it was difficult to see more than a few yards in any direction due to the overgrown foliage.

Once inside the steel skeleton of the greenhouse, Yuri and Dimitri stopped to catch their breath. Wheezing heavily, the cousins leaned on each other, slowly calming their racing hearts and fighting to regain control of their breathing. The interior of the greenhouse was relatively well protected due to the density of the tree and brush cover around it, giving the pair some small measure of comfort that they might not be immediately spotted by whoever or whatever had been chasing after them.

Yuri abruptly collapsed to the ground next to Dimitri, still gasping as he fell. Tired and sore from their run, Yuri's legs had simply given out and he sat on the rough gravel and patches of broken glass as he rubbed his calves. Dimitri wasn't faring much better and knelt down next to Yuri, putting his hand on Yuri's shoulder.

"Are you okay?" Dimitri's voice was hoarse as he struggled to squeeze the words out. Yuri nodded in response, keeping his head tucked low as he spoke.

"Yeah, I'm okay. I feel like crap, though."

Dimitri looked around the greenhouse, then stood up and dragged a broken table over to Yuri. "Come on, better to sit up here than on the ground. Probably less radiation that way." Yuri nodded in thanks and pulled himself up on the table alongside his cousin. Dimitri pulled the Kalash off of his back and laid it alongside him on the table. He gingerly pulled back the sleeve of his coat, wincing at the sight of his arm under his flashlight. Bits of grit and gravel were visible in the wound that stretched from his wrist to his elbow on the underside of his arm. While the injury wasn't serious, it was painful and Dimitri could already see some oozing around the edges and center of the wound.

When the boys had come into the city, they had left most of their belongings in the car, carrying only small shoulder bags with them that had enough food for two meals and the most basic medical supplies. A few antiseptic wipes, small bandages and a few feet of gauze was all that was available between the both of them. After Yuri saw Dimitri's arm in the light, he insisted on helping cover it up to keep it from getting infected. Dimitri protested but eventually gave in to his cousin's tenacity.

After wiping Dimitri's arm down with an antiseptic wipe, Yuri used a second one to pick out as many pieces of grit and dirt from the wound as possible. Dimitri then held on to the gauze as Yuri wrapped it around the injury, securing it in place with the adhesive bandages at both ends. While the dressing wasn't perfect, it was enough to protect Dimitri's arm from getting irritated by his jacket and to – hopefully – keep it from getting infected.

Dimitri jumped down from the table and carefully slid his jacket sleeve down over his arm. He turned to his cousin to try and decide what to do next, but Yuri spoke first.

"We should leave tonight, Dimitri." Yuri slid off the table, wobbling slightly as he moved his legs. "Something was after us and I don't want to meet it again."

Yuri was surprised to hear his cousin's response. "You're right. This is way too dangerous." Dimitri started to walk toward the opposite end of the greenhouse from where they had entered. "Let's get out here and get out into the fields. Then we can just go south and get back to the car before morning."

Yuri followed Dimitri along through the greenhouse, doing his best to avoid touching the plants that had taken over the structure. As he and Dimitri neared the opposite end of the building, Yuri idly glanced down at his open jacket, spotting the radiation meter dangling from his chest. He stifled a yelp as he grabbed the meter and turned it upright, blinking several times to make sure he wasn't imagining things.

"Dimitri!" Yuri whispered loudly, desperately calling his cousin over to return to him. Dimitri rushed back, looking at the radiation meter Yuri held aloft.

"What the hell?"

The meter was well within the yellow zone and rising, a level that wasn't lethal to humans, but soon would be if they didn't get out of the area quickly. Yuri ran back toward the section of the greenhouse they had entered, watching the meter as he went. With each step he took, the meter's rise gradually began to slow until it stopped, halfway through the yellow section but still below the orange and red ones. Dimitri pulled his radiation meter off of his shirt as well, comparing it to Yuri's.

"Mine's doing the same thing. Damn!"

Yuri kept staring at the meter, wondering if it was going to spike upward again. A moment passed in silence as the cousins each watched their radiation meters until Yuri finally spoke again. "Why aren't they moving anymore?"

Dimitri shook his head. "There must be a pocket of moss or something back there that we didn't see. Damn!" Dimitri cursed several more times, angry at himself at the danger they had both just been placed in.

In Prip'Yat, one of the most dangerous spots to be was on or near a patch of moss. Moss, it turned out, had a nasty habit of absorbing extremely high doses of radiation from the soil, which turned it into a deathtrap if you stood on it for too long. There were other hotspots of radiation around the city, but surrounded by greenery, it made sense that a patch of moss would go unnoticed for long enough to irradiate them.

"Come on, Yuri, let's get out of here." Dimitri pushed through the side of the greenhouse, fighting with the tree limbs as he exited. When Yuri came through next, he nearly ran into the back of Dimitri, who was standing rigid outside the structure, not moving a single muscle on his body. Yuri began to move around Dimitri and tease him for his laziness when he looked up and saw what Dimitri was staring at.

Off in the distance, toward one edge of the city, red glowing eyes shone at them again as a dark shape stumbled along, alternating between moving slow and low to the ground and running along at a greater height. The shape wasn't moving toward the cousins, but it was circling the edge of the city, cutting off their chances at escaping directly to their vehicle.

Yuri felt panic rise in his throat and he turned to run, pulling Dimitri along with him. "Come on! Move!" He hissed at his older cousin, dislodging Dimitri from his stare and causing him to break into a run as well.

Chapter Twelve
Iosif Seleznev | Lucas Pokrov

The interior of the building was quiet like the rest of the city, though the silence was more unnerving than it should have been. Every bootstep, every breath, and every aberrant noise from the soldiers' equipment was more potential for their positions to be given away. Broken glass and rubble from the interior of the building blocked their paths, forcing them to go even slower than they had when they first entered the building.

The main floor of the building behind the desk was a labyrinth of rooms. Filled with everything from chairs to examination tables, it was disorienting in the darkness, even to the seasoned soldiers. After entering the building, Lucas switched from his SVD to a sawed-off shotgun that he kept strapped to his back. The weapon was light and versatile, capable of holding a total of six shells with a length of less than two feet. Although it lacked both night vision and thermal imaging devices, it was equipped with an under-barrel tactical light that shone in both white and red in varying degrees of brightness.

After several minutes of searching the upper floors, Lucas whispered into his microphone. "I'm going to check if there's a basement level."

A single click came back over the radio, indicating that Iosif had received Lucas's message and approved of the decision. Lucas backtracked through the facility, seeing Iosif's dim light several rooms away as he passed into the main entryway again. To one side sat a door with a stairway symbol on it that Lucas carefully pushed open, keeping his shotgun level in front of him the entire time. The stairwell was in good condition, though it had a significant amount of debris piled in it from the upper floor. From what Lucas could see, the upper floor had caved in some time ago, making it impossible to proceed upstairs.

Without hesitation Lucas moved down the stairs, switching from corner to corner with precision, exactly as he had trained for countless hours. He didn't like moving into unknown territory alone, but unless he and Iosif wanted to be in the city for the full three days allotted to them, they would need to start speeding up their investigation.

At the bottom of the stairwell, Lucas stopped and switched off his light, allowing his eyes to acclimate to the darkness below. After a good thirty seconds of staring into the dark, Lucas switched on the flashlight on his shotgun, illuminating the stairwell with a thin beam of blood red light. The red light would help preserve Lucas's night vision and give him some measure of stealth that a normal flashlight beam would be unable to provide. After taking a deep breath, Lucas pushed through the door of the stairwell, stepping into the basement hallway beyond.

The layout of the lower level of the building was more spacious than the main floor had been. Fewer rooms with more square footage made it easier to navigate, especially since the rooms were all laid out around one central hall that led directly from the stairwell to the back of the building. Lucas swept from room to room in a precision manner, working to clear them as fast as possible. When he had reached the halfway point in the hallway, his radio sparked to life and Iosif's voice came through.

"I finished my sweep upstairs. There's nothing here. I'm heading down to your position."

Lucas tapped the microphone button once in acknowledgement of Iosif's message and slowed down his sweep, waiting for his partner to arrive. When they were together, Lucas stuck to the right side of the hall while Iosif covered the left, the two of them working in tandem to go through the rooms on opposite sides of the hallway.

Each of the rooms so far was devoid of movement and life, though they were far from empty. More furniture and equipment filled the large chambers, speaking volumes about the people and activities that had once taken place here. The building appeared to be a type of medical or research facility, with abundant surgical chambers and research laboratory facilities. Most of the glassware and equipment had long ago been torn apart by vandals, but enough bits and pieces remained to paint a stark picture of what the building must have been like before the disaster.

Lucas and Iosif approached the end of the corridor where it branched off to the right, each of them scanning the area with their weapons and tactical lights. Out of nowhere a noise from around the corner of the hall caught their attention. They both dropped to their knees and pressed their bodies against the walls, checking into nearby rooms and down the hallway for the source of the disturbance.

Around a corner in the hall, the noise came again, louder this time and it was accompanied by the distinct sound of movement. Lucas and Iosif both stood and glanced at each other. Iosif jerked his head forward to prompt Lucas to take the point position. The noise grew louder as Lucas glanced around the corner, catching sight of a black shape that vanished in the darkness of the hall. He jerked his body around the corner, bringing his weapon to bear in the direction that the shape had disappeared as Iosif brought up the rear. After a few more seconds of activity, the noise abruptly vanished, causing the soldiers to move even slower down the corridor.

Several minutes passed as the pair checked every room in the short side hallway, coming up empty at the end of it. Iosif glanced into one of the rooms near where the movement had vanished, spying a hole that led up through the ceiling onto the main floor. He slowly circled the hole, keeping his rifle trained on it while Lucas watched.

"You think whatever it was went through there?" Lucas whispered to Iosif, unsure of what to do next.

Iosif looked at the hole for several more seconds then turned and headed back through the door. "Who knows? It got away, though, whatever it was. It left more evidence that it was here, though."

Lucas turned to follow Iosif when a glint on the floor caught his eye. Another pile of the strange substance lay quivering on the floor, moving back and forth ever so slightly in time with the vibration from Iosif's footsteps. Lucas gulped nervously and followed Iosif back out into the hall, up the stairs and out to the front of the building.

"It can't have gotten far. Sweep left, I'll go right." Iosif gave the order tersely to Lucas, his voice coming through Lucas's earpiece strained and nervous. The pressure of the tight quarters and strange environment of the city and its abandoned buildings was starting to get to Iosif, who longed for an enemy he could fight openly instead of chasing around in the darkness. Lucas swerved to the left of the building, following it around to the back. They both paused at the back of the building, searching the area with their scopes for any signs of life.

"There! On the thermal, I see something!" A hundred yards down the road a distinct heat impression on the pavement was fading rapidly, turning from a pale yellow to a light blue before Lucas's eyes. He looked over the scope to verify the position, then began to head forward with Iosif providing cover from the rear. Moments later, the pair reached the location of the heat source, which had already vanished. There was no other evidence that anything had been at the location, but with more real proof of another entity in the area with them, Iosif and Lucas both grew instantly more alert and on guard.

"How big was the signature?" Iosif's voice was a mere whisper over the radio, not wanting to give away their position to anyone who might be listening nearby.

Lucas swiped his finger in an oval shape on the ground, outlining a rough estimate for how big the heat signature had shown up on the scope. It was about twice the length of Lucas's hand and located right in the middle of the road leading north through the city. No other heat signatures were nearby, but Iosif was still concerned for their safety. He signaled Lucas to move to the opposite side of the roadway again and then took up position on the western edge, moving forward through the bushes with lightning precision.

Speed was a necessity at this point, with the soldiers growing closer to finding the source of the noises, sounds, foreign objects and the heat signature they had found. Safety was never compromised, despite the rapidity of their movement, and the pair soon found themselves lying in a field, sweeping the area ahead with the scopes in hopes of spotting any movement.

Virtually buried in grass that extended almost over his entire body, Lucas was incredibly thankful for the masks that he and Iosif wore, and he tried not to think about the radioactive particles that he was picking up just by lying down in the grass for a few minutes. A stand of trees and thick brush was ahead, and Lucas's radiation meter was beginning to go wild, signaling that pockets of intense radiation were near.

Iosif confirmed this on his radiation detector, then he brought up a map on his GPS unit, checking the area they were in for any known radiation hotspots. After looking at the map for several seconds he frowned and spoke over the radio.

"Lucas, give me an estimated range to the hotspot ahead of us."

Lucas held his radiation meter above his head, sweeping it from left to right in front of him. "I'd guess maybe twenty-five to thirty meters."

"Damn. There's nothing on the map up there." Iosif punched a button on his GPS to turn it off before jamming it angrily back into his vest pocket. Sweat poured down on his face inside his mask, obscuring his vision and making him blink several times to clear the moisture away. Lucas remained silent, waiting for Iosif to give the word on what to do.

"Listen up, Lucas. Whatever's out there may be capable of generating a radioactive signature strong enough to show up at distance on our meters. Advance slowly, spread out another ten meters and continue moving forward."

Lucas nodded in response, pushed himself to his knees and began to advance, crouching in the tall grasses as he and Iosif made their way toward the trees and the radiation signature ahead.

Chapter Thirteen
Yuri Volkov | Dimitri Alexeiev

Darting between buildings, Yuri and Dimitri ran back through the city the way they had come in, down the road and moving east through the apartment buildings. Whatever the red-eyed shape was, they didn't see it pursuing them. Once they were a few hundred yards from the greenhouse they broke into a run, throwing caution and stealth to the wind.

Moments later the pair reached the main square of the city, passing by the Palace of Culture and the arch. Dimitri thought briefly about trying to hide in one of the buildings in the square again, but decided that they were better off in the open. *At least out here,* he thought, *there's less chance of us being surprised by that thing.*

"Where now?" Yuri panted at Dimitri as they ran. Their car was far to the west, beyond the area where they had spotted the creature. To the southeast lay the Chernobyl power plant, though it was farther away than either of the cousins wanted to travel. There wasn't anything there anyway, except for vast amounts of radiation and rusted construction equipment. South of the city along the main road were checkpoints set up by the military to guard against unauthorized intrusions into the city.

The first checkpoint was substantially farther away than Chernobyl, a few kilometers from their current position. While the checkpoint would take a long time to reach, it would be manned by a few military guards who could help the cousins. This would mean admitting that they were trespassing in the city and potentially be thrown in jail or fined, but anything was preferable to spending more time in the city with the thing that was after them.

Before Dimitri could answer, a shot rang out behind them, far away at the edge of the city. Both of the boys froze in their tracks, their lungs aching as they held their breath to listen for any more gunfire. They didn't have to wait long, as several more shots followed the first. The gunfire echoed through the pavement and buildings of Prip'Yat, making it difficult to tell exactly where it was coming from. Panicked, Dimitri grabbed Yuri's arm, pulling him toward a nearby building.

"Shit! It's the military!"

Yuri hurried alongside Dimitri, craning his head back and forth to try and narrow down the location of the shots. "Do you think they're after us?"

Dimitri shook his head, uncertain about all of the events of the night. "How would I know? We need to hide, though. If they find us, we're screwed!"

"What if... what if they're after that thing we saw?" Yuri was hesitant to bring up the topic of the red-eyed apparition they had seen in the city, but it seemed just as likely that the gunfire was directed toward the thing as it was at them. Several more shots rang out, this time much closer to the boys' position. Ducking low as they ran, Dimitri and Yuri ran inside the large hospital building that was closest to them, scrambling to find a place to hide.

Before turning a corner to travel down a flight of stairs, Yuri glanced back out the front door of the hospital, straining to see any sign of the source of the shots. In the distance, beyond the far apartment buildings, the pair of red eyes was visible along with the dark shape. It moved swiftly forward, and with each shot Yuri heard, a small flash of light was visible near to the shape.

Yuri ran down the stairs, informing his cousin of what he had seen.

"Shit." Dimitri muttered. "They must be after that thing. It's coming this way?"

"I don't know. I think so, though." Yuri had only looked out the front door for a few seconds, and he had no way of knowing for sure whether or not the thing had spotted them entering the building or not. Caution demanded that they assume that it was chasing after them, though, so they hurried through the corridors of the hospital, searching for a room that was secure enough to hide in.

Most of the doors in the hospital were still on their hinges, though about half of them had their locks broken or their handles smashed. A moment of frantic searching passed without results, then Yuri pushed open a pair of thick steel doors leading into a large open room. Rows of seats were arranged in a high half circle around the center of the room where a damaged surgical table sat. Broken lights dangled from above the table, their shadows lending an eerie ambience to the room in the glow of Yuri and Dimitri's flashlights.

"Quick, up the stairs! We'll hide back there!" Dimitri pointed up the side of the theater-style seating to a small room that overlooked both the seats and the surgical area. Hurrying up the stairs, Dimitri and Yuri scrambled to get into the room as quickly as possible. A few chairs lay toppled on the floor, remnants of the control room for the surgical theater where technicians could monitor operations without being in the way of either the doctors or the students in the seats below. Dimitri slid down on the floor next to Yuri, pulling the door to the technician's booth closed behind him.

As their breathing slowed, Yuri and Dimitri's ears grew used to the silence in the room. Gunfire continued to echo far in the distance, sounding like the faint popping of firecrackers through the thick walls of the hospital. Yuri whispered to Dimitri, fearful for what might happen next.

"It sounds like they're still outside. Maybe they won't find us down here."

"I'm more worried about what might be chasing us, and about my arm. We'd be lucky if the soldiers found us." Dimitri lifted the dressing on his arm, wincing at the pain. His wound was inflamed around the edges, signifying that an infection had started to set in. While it was still treatable, he needed to get to a doctor soon before it got any worse.

Yuri tried to look at Dimitri's arm but was pushed back as Dimitri covered it back up, not wanting to cause undue worry in his younger cousin. "It's fine, don't worry about it. I just need to see a doctor soon."

Commotion from the hallway outside the door made the pair grow silent again as they waited to see what would happen next. Minutes ticked by without any sound aside from a scratching that seemed to travel back and forth down the hallway. The scratching was occasionally accompanied by the sound of footsteps. The gunshots had ceased briefly before the noises began, and Yuri began to wonder if the sounds in the hallway could be the soldiers they had heard firing outside.

"Yuri, do you have the Kalash?" Dimitri's question came as a surprise to Yuri, who assumed that Dimitri had held on to the weapon.

"No, you had it, remember?"

Dimitri was quiet, and Yuri tried to remember the last time he had seen his cousin with the rifle. Realization dawned on Yuri as he recalled their brief rest at the greenhouse, where Dimitri had taken off the rifle to be more comfortable as they sat down.

Before Yuri could pose a question to Dimitri, his cousin was already pushing himself up. He crept out the door and moved silently down the stairs, ignoring Yuri's wild hand and facial gestures begging him to stop. With his arm infected and in pain, Dimitri knew he had to take a risk to try and get both Yuri and himself out of the city as quickly as possible. If there were soldiers in the building, then it was very possible that he could reason with them. Without the rifle he would be vulnerable to whatever had been chasing them, but despite the lack of protection, Dimitri had made up his mind about what he had to do.

Dimitri pressed his ear against the door of the surgical theater, listening to the noises outside. The scraping and the footsteps still reverberated down the hallway, now closer than ever. With a deep breath, Dimitri slowly pushed open the door, peeking out into the hallway. The beam of his flashlight cut through the darkness of the hall, though it didn't reveal anything out of the ordinary. The source of the sounds was close, but not visible from the angle he was at. Dimitri looked back at the technician's booth where Yuri was crouching in the doorway, watching Dimitri's every move.

As Dimitri walked through the door, letting it close slowly behind him, Yuri noticed that the noises in the hall stopped. He heard Dimitri's muffled speech, then was shocked as several gunshots rang out. The shots were very close by, and sounded as if they were coming from the hallway. A few seconds later, an enormous crash came from outside the room and Yuri ducked down instinctively, feeling the vibrations from the crash all the way at the back of the room. More gunfire erupted from inside the building, followed by silence and then the most gut-wrenching sound Yuri had heard in his life.

The scream had unquestionably emanated from the mouth of Dimitri, though it was unnatural and guttural. The scream rose in pitch over the few seconds it lasted, before it finally cut off with a faint gurgle. Several more seconds passed in slow motion as Yuri agonized over the sounds he had just heard. When the next round of gunfire erupted, Yuri was slower to react, his senses dulled by the raw emotions overwhelming him.

A distant yell followed the gunfire, then more gunfire and finally another large crash. The cacophony of sounds was a blur to Yuri, who failed to pay any attention to them. Slumped behind the desk in the technician's booth, Yuri pulled his knees up to his chest and buried his head in his legs, fighting to choke back tears.

Chapter Fourteen
Iosif Seleznev | Lucas Pokrov

Though their time so far in the city had been moderately eventful, nothing that Iosif and Lucas had encountered so far had prepared them for the events that began to unfold before their eyes. The pair of soldiers moved toward the radiation signature together, alternating between crawling through the thick grass and crouching to get a better angle to perform thermal and infrared scans on the area.

While nothing was appearing on any visual, thermal or infrared scans that they did, both Lucas's and Iosif's radiation meters were still going wild, indicating that an intensely radioactive source was just in front of them.

"Cover me while I move up," Iosif whispered through his microphone as he moved forward through the grass. He held his radiation meter up in front of him like a shield while keeping the rifle steady, pointed forward to the cluster of trees just ahead. Lucas moved perpendicular to Iosif and then lay back down in the grass, extending the bipod that was attached to the front of his SVD. While the SVD didn't normally come with any type of stabilization mechanism, Lucas preferred to have one as it made long periods of waiting much more tolerable.

Through the thermal scope on the SVD, Lucas could see Iosif advancing forward, stopping every few feet to wave the radiation meter in front of him. A few moments passed before Iosif's voice came through on the radio.

"The radiation levels aren't getting any stronger yet. The source must be on the other side of these trees. I'm advancing forward."

The light orange form of Iosif began to break up on the thermal scope as he walked through the trees. After just a few feet, his body appeared as nothing more than thin slivers of orange that happened to show through the cracks in the foliage and tree trunks.

"I've lost sight of you on the thermal." Lucas switched to his infrared scope, though that didn't offer any better results than the thermal scope, in terms of keeping an eye on Iosif. There was no response to Lucas's statement, and he began to worry about the status of his partner when the radio finally cracked and Iosif's hurried voice came through again.

"Get up here now!" Iosif's tone was worried, though it didn't sound like he was in trouble. Nonetheless, Lucas did as he was instructed, jumping up and running full tilt toward the stand of trees where Iosif had vanished. The group of trees was several meters thick, a small grouping out on the edge of the city. Just beyond them lay what appeared to be another grouping of trees. As he drew closer, though, Lucas could see that it wasn't just trees. A variety of flora had grown up around a metal structure, masking its original form.

On his thermal scope, Lucas could see Iosif's outline just inside the structure. He was kneeling on the ground, examining something in front of him. "Coming in." Lucas warned Iosif of his imminent arrival and then jogged forward, turning his head back and forth to ensure he and Iosif were alone. After he pushed through the trees he nearly stumbled into Iosif, who had backed up to the edge of the structure.

"Careful, don't go forward any farther."

A steady beeping in Lucas's ear told him the reason for Iosif's warning. Lucas's radiation meter was in the red zone, indicating that radiation levels in their vicinity were at high enough levels to be deadly. Lucas looked around at the interior of the structure, momentarily distracted by the size of it. It looked like it had once been a greenhouse, though all of the glass had been broken out years ago. The plants in the greenhouse could certainly give off a larger amount of radiation than in other spots, but the readings here were equivalent to what you could find closer in to the Chernobyl disaster site itself.

"Shouldn't we get out of here?" Lucas motioned toward the end of the greenhouse with his head. Iosif looked over at him and replied.

"No, we're safe for the moment. Our suits will block this stuff. Besides, it's incredibly localized. The scanners are picking it up from a distance due to their sensitivity, but it won't do much to you until you get right into it. There," Iosif pointed down at the ground a few feet away. "See that indentation? That's where it's coming from."

Lucas crouched next to Iosif and directed his flashlight toward the spot Iosif had pointed out. In the middle of the red light was a large indent in the gravel and dirt, a few inches deep, several feet long and several feet wide. Lucas pulled out his radiation meter and waved it around, confirming that the indentation was, indeed, the source of the intense radioactivity.

"What the hell is it?"

Iosif didn't reply to Lucas, but walked around the indent, through what used to be a doorway in the greenhouse and into the next section. Lucas followed behind him, still confused over what they were witnessing. Iosif stopped at a table in the structure, examining an object that was lying on top of the table. He turned to Lucas and pointed at the object. "Now we have two problems."

Lucas went to the table to examine the object, gasping as he saw what it was. He stared at the object for a few seconds before his radio cracked. "Make that three." Lucas watched as Iosif knelt down again, examining the dirt on the ground. Lucas crouched next to him and watched as Iosif used his finger to trace the faint outlines of two pairs of footprints that disappeared in the thick gravel.

"So what are we hunting? A man or a beast?"

Iosif shook his head. "This isn't right. None of this is right. No one is supposed to be here but us." He looked back at the table where the AK still sat, forgotten by a recent visitor to the greenhouse. "We're not after whoever left that." Iosif pointed at the gun, then jabbed a thumb over his back at the section of the greenhouse containing the indentation. "We're after whatever left that."

Lucas stood, frustrated with Iosif's cryptic comments. "Sir, I know I'm not quite as experienced as you, but I'm not wet behind the ears, either. If you want me to do my job as your partner, I need to know what you know."

Iosif didn't respond to Lucas's demand at first. He continued to kneel on the ground, touching the footprints lightly as though he could pry the identity of their creator out of the dirt they had been inscribed in.

Finally he stood and sat on the table next to Lucas, cradling his rifle in his arms. He sighed deeply, causing a plume of mist to cloud the interior of his mask. "This is all too familiar. Before you were promoted to the special operations unit, I worked on an operation in southern China five years ago. It was a large team, a total of six of us plus two scientists we were tasked to guard."

"Guard duty?" Lucas stood in front of Iosif, still holding his gun at the ready in case of an attack. "Since when are special operations members used for guard duty?"

Iosif nodded. "Yes, guard duty. It was highly unusual, but what made it more so was how we were outfitted. We were armed to the teeth. Hell, even the scientists were armed and armored like they were going into a warzone."

Lucas struggled to remember the state of the world in the Middle East five years ago. "There wasn't a war going on there, though."

"Just shut up and let me finish." Iosif's voice was strained and his body tense. He began to speed up his story, glancing around nervously as he did so.

"We were dropped off in the middle of the desert under the cover of night to, as we were told, 'investigate rumors of unusual activity near a suspected nuclear weapons facility.'" Iosif nearly spat in disgust, then remembered at the last moment that he was wearing the mask. "It was a massacre. The facility was completely deserted and we lost both scientists and four of the special operations team before we got out. The other one who got out died of his injuries a few hours later. Want to know what he died from?"

Lucas nodded as Iosif eyed him.

"Catastrophic radiation poisoning. That's what the doctors said."

"Well, you were near a nuclear facility, right? That's the one that the Americans ended up bombing if I remember correctly."

Iosif nodded again. "You do remember correctly. Our leaders contacted the Americans and spoke with their leaders. Twelve hours later the Americans saturated the Chinese facility with hundreds of their biggest bombs and we sent in ground troops to clean up the mess. The Chinese never batted an eye at us, that's how unusual this was."

Lucas shifted on his feet. "So what's this got to do with this op?"

"I'm getting there. I said the other survivor died from radiation poisoning. What do you think happened to the other six?"

"Radiation poisoning, I would assume."

Iosif turned his head to the side, staring into space as he spoke. "If only. I saw two of them die, one of the scientists and another of our team. The scientist was the first to go. He was next to us, in a room inside the facility we were defending against a few squads of Chinese soldiers we encountered. I saw him…" Iosif hesitated, trying to piece together his memory in a coherent way.

"It was a shadow, some kind of thing that tore him apart, literally ripped him to shreds. He didn't have time to scream before it was all over. His body armor did nothing to stop it, either. Standard procedure is to retrieve a body from an operational area and return it, but there was nothing left to retrieve unless you used a sponge."

Lucas started to ask a question when Iosif raised his hand, silencing him. He cocked his head, listening as he slowly rose from the table.

"Do you hear that?" Iosif whispered through the radio. Lucas had been distracted by the story, enough that it took him a moment to pick up on what Iosif was hearing. A faint shuffling in the distance, some scratching and footsteps came through very faintly. On alert, both soldiers readied their weapons and crept through the rest of the greenhouse, moving toward the source of the noise. Lucas's mind was still reeling from the revelations Iosif had explained, but he still didn't know whether to believe the story or not.

A few feet from the exit to the greenhouse, Iosif suddenly ran toward the edge of the structure, shouldering his way through the saplings and bushes that had grown around it. Lucas pushed through as well, just as Iosif raised his rifle, firing into the distance, toward the city.

"Shoot, damn you! Shoot!" Iosif hissed at Lucas, who raised his rifle and looked down the scope. The infrared scope was still engaged, and Lucas couldn't make out anything in the distance that looked like a threat. He switched the SVD over to the thermal scope with a flick of the wrist and raised it up again. This time, a massive heat bloom was visible, moving away from them with a frightening speed.

Lucas squeezed the SVD's trigger several times, sending a half dozen rounds down toward the target. He couldn't tell from this distance if they had impacted, but the heat signature didn't stop moving, regardless of whether or not Iosif's and his rounds were hitting their target. After several more shots, the signature disappeared behind a building, vanishing from Lucas's thermal scope.

Iosif took off at a run, waving his arm for Lucas to follow behind him. Moments later, the pair stopped again, checking the area for signs of the thing they had been firing at. To Lucas's surprise, the ground gave no evidence that the thing had passed through, with no footprints visible on the thermal scope despite the creature's huge size. Listening carefully, though, they heard the footsteps and rustling again. Just as they started to follow in the direction of the noise, Lucas saw a dark shadow appear in front of a distant building, go up the steps and vanish into the entrance.

Lucas pointed ahead of them. "There, it went into the hospital!" Iosif nodded as he watched the shadow disappear. Iosif took off at a sprint, making a beeline for the hospital entrance as Lucas followed close behind.

Breathing heavily, Iosif and Lucas entered the building and weaved their way through the hospital. Its layout was similar to the building they had visited previously, though it was much larger in size and in the number of rooms it held. The path of the soldiers was clear, though, as they continued to pick up intermittent spots of radiation on the floor and walls of the hospital corridors. Iosif warned Lucas not to fire at their target until they had a clear line of sight again, despite the temptation to shoot at the brief glimpses of orange in the thermal scope as it ducked around corners and through holes in the walls.

"Don't forget that there are other people here. If they get in the way, shoot them, but there's no need to recklessly kill civilians." Lucas agreed with Iosif's sentiment, but the younger soldier was eager to see their hunt complete so that he could begin to get answers to the questions bubbling up inside. Spetsnaz training instilled strict discipline into its members, more so than troops in the normal ranks of the military received. Lucas was bucking against that training now, disturbed by both their mission and by Iosif's brief story in the greenhouse.

A gentle thud broke Lucas from his thoughts and he looked at Iosif. "That sounded like a door closing."

"This thing doesn't use doors. Christ, the other people must be in the building. It's hunting them."

A second, softer impact came as Iosif was speaking and they both strained to hear where it had come from. "Below us?" Lucas said with a whisper, pointing down the hall at a stairwell.

Debris crashed down from the ceiling in front of the two officers as Iosif started his reply, cutting him off before he could begin to speak. Through a hole in the ceiling, a dark shape fell to the ground, deftly ducking to the side to avoid the hail of gunfire unleashed upon it by the two soldiers. The shadow tore at the wall with long, savage claws, pulling itself along the side of Iosif and landing behind him.

Lucas and Iosif turned to fire at the shadow, but their quick reactions were no match for the beast. Standing a few feet away, Lucas watched in horror as the shadow reached out for Iosif, its long muscular arms masked by wispy tendrils of darkness. Iosif's finger instinctively pulled the trigger on his rifle and a burst of bullets tore through the shadow. It made no noise as it absorbed the gunfire, seemingly unaffected by the steam of depleted uranium and lead.

Blood red eyes stared into Iosif's mask, meeting his gaze head on. The seconds he spent in the shadow's grasp stretched in slow motion. Rows of black teeth glinted in the light of Lucas and Iosif's guns as the shadow stretched open the upper portion of its frame. Using both its limbs and its teeth, it rended Iosif's body, tearing his head from his shoulders and splitting his torso apart in the center.

Lucas screamed as he fired his SVD, squeezing the trigger multiple times until the weapon clicked, indicating that it was out of ammunition. The creature paid Lucas no mind as it fled down the hall, jumping up and then crashing down, forming a gaping hole in the floor. In shock, Lucas stood stark still, unsure of what to do next. His training had prepared him to face death and atrocities on every scale, but never to face a foe the likes of this.

Lucas was shaken from his stupor by the sound of a second scream that came from the floor below. Turning around, he ran toward the stairwell, releasing the empty magazine from his SVD and replacing it with one containing bullets with bright orange tips. Along with standard armor-piercing rounds, Lucas had brought several magazines containing high-explosive rounds, capable of blowing a hole the size of a car in a steel wall.

Let's see how you handle this, you bastard!

Chapter Fifteen
Lucas Pokrov | Yuri Volkov

As the largest medical building in the city, the main hospital was where the majority of the injured citizens and workers were brought after the explosion of reactor four. There were three wings in the main hospital building, each with its own complicated set of corridors and rooms. The condition of the hospital was the same as the rest of the city as it too had suffered under the ravages of both vandals and time.

Rotten floorboards, crumbling walls, peeling paint and sagging roofs were only the beginning of the building's troubles. Smaller wildlife in the city had found comfort among the leftover medical supplies, leading to rat and mice nests being scattered throughout the building. Most of the medical equipment was scavenged by thieves in the months following the disaster, though this situation had a certain irony as the supplies did more harm than good due to the radiation that had contaminated them.

The darkness combined with the dilapidated condition of the hospital made Lucas's task none the easier as he ran forward. A splatter of blood had been thrown across his mask by Iosif's death, though Lucas made no move to wipe it away. Through the red color he saw only anger and destruction as his rage became the focal point through which he concentrated.

Coming out of the stairwell and into the basement, Lucas saw a shadowy figure ram through a pair of double doors, pushing its way into a large chamber beyond. Lucas picked up his speed as he ran down the hall, his finger instinctively brushing against the trigger of his SVD. *All I need is a good shot, and you're fucked.* In the back of Lucas's mind, he wondered whether this was true. Both he and Iosif had dumped at least two dozen rounds each into the apparition, all without effect. The high-explosive rounds were different, though, or so Lucas hoped.

Inside the surgical theater, Yuri's heart began to skip beats as terror overwhelmed him. While he didn't see the shadow creature enter into the room, he could feel its presence and hear the soft 'tick tick tick' of its feet on the floor. The scratching and rustling of the creature made his brain scream and his baser instincts threatened to take over. *Run! Run, you fool, before it's too late!* Yuri held still, though, remembering the screams from outside the room that proved that this creature was not something that could be easily escaped.

The sound of soft breathing reached Yuri's ears and he realized that the creature had somehow come all the way up the stairs of the theater. The flashlight at Yuri's feet was still on, he noticed, and he quietly fumbled with it, desperate to turn it off in a vain attempt to conceal his location. As the beam passed over his shirt, he noticed his radiation meter. The small tag was already into the orange zone and rising rapidly after remaining still since they had escaped the greenhouse. Yuri dropped the flashlight to the ground in shock, mesmerized by the rapidly changing color of his radiation meter.

A sudden scraping from outside the technician's booth accompanied the clatter of the flashlight, distracting Yuri from the radiation tag and bringing him back to reality. Yuri took a deep breath and picked the flashlight up again, squeezing the base of it hard in his right hand. *I won't go down without a fight,* he thought, though he knew that any resistance he could put up to the creature would be utterly futile.

Yuri stood up from the floor of the technician's booth, and turned to face the shadow that stood before him. Before the beam of the flashlight could pass over the creature, a shout came from the front of the surgical theater, distracting the creature towering over Yuri and causing it to whip around to face the source of the noise.

"Hey you! Catch!" Standing in the doorway of the surgical theater, Lucas held his SVD firmly against his shoulder. His breathing was rapid but in control and he allowed his training and instincts as a sniper to take over. Time slowed as the laser beam from the bottom of the SVD's barrel shone across the head of the shadow, reflecting in its twin red eyes and glinting off of its bared teeth.

Out of the corner of Lucas's eye he saw the glint of Yuri's flashlight and said a quick silent prayer that whoever was holding the light wouldn't be harmed. The shadow began to move toward Lucas, furious at his intrusion on its hunt. To Lucas, it felt like he had been standing in the doorway of the room for hours, but only a few seconds had gone by. His gloved hand wrapped around the trigger of the SVD, squeezing in time with his breathing to avoid any unnecessary kick of the rifle. While the beating of his heart and the exhalation and inhalation of his breaths were unlikely to affect the bullet's trajectory at such close range, he didn't want to take any chances with the creature.

The SVD's firing mechanism engaged precisely with Lucas's squeeze of the trigger, causing the round in the chamber of the rifle to be expelled at high velocity out of the end of the barrel. The orange-tipped round flew at the creature, striking it squarely between its red eyes. For a split second, Lucas thought he might have grabbed the wrong magazine from his pouch. A grim smile spread across his face, though, when the round activated, causing a massive explosion to bloom out of the creature's head.

While the shadow beast didn't make any audible noise to show its rage and pain, both Yuri and Lucas winced as it staggered back, the high-explosive round having done serious harm to it. Not waiting to see whether or not one round would be enough, Lucas squeezed the trigger again, expelling round after round into the beast. Each impact caused a new explosion of light, sound and fire to emanate from the beast's body. With each explosion the two men winced in pain, affected by the creature's reactions to the bullets in ways that they didn't fully understand.

Before Lucas heard the rifle click to indicate that it was empty, he had already dropped the empty magazine on the floor and slapped in a new one. His right hand ran along the side of the weapon, chambering a new round from the magazine into place with a metallic clang. For the briefest of seconds, the room was dark and quiet, the flashlight belonging to Yuri having been switched off as he cowered in the technician's booth, covering his ears from the onslaught.

Lucas squeezed the trigger again, though this time the results were less spectacular. Instead of impacting upon the shadow creature, the round passed through one of the rotting walls at the back of the theater, causing an explosion in the next room as it finally impacted on a solid object. Lucas pulled his finger back from firing another round, panicked as he realized that the creature had disappeared in the few seconds it took him to change magazines in his rifle.

The thermal scope to the rifle was flipped up in a flash and Lucas peered through it, twisting and turning as he scanned the room for any signs of activity. Finally his gaze rested on the tall ceiling above the seats where the shadow had stood not seconds before. A gaping hole had been torn in the ceiling and the edges were white hot on his scope, indicating that the creature had somehow managed to leap two stories into the air through the roof onto the next floor.

Lucas kept his rifle trained on the hole as he maneuvered his way to the stairs leading up to the technician's booth in the theater. As the ringing in Lucas's ears began to die down, silence once again reigned in the hospital. After a moment, a shuffle from behind Lucas caused him to turn around, training the rifle on the source. A teenager who looked to be no older than eighteen was standing in front of him, staring at him in amazement.

Yuri shone his light at Lucas, marveling at the sight in front of him. Dressed in all black, loaded for bear with weapons and equipment, the masked man who had just saved his life was an impressive sight to behold, even with his rifle pointed directly at Yuri's face. Yuri quickly raised his hands, holding the flashlight in his quivering grip high above his head. He struggled to speak, begging for his life from the man who had just saved it.

"Please don't kill me! I'm sorry we came here! Just please, don't kill me!"

Chapter Sixteen
Lucas Pokrov | Yuri Volkov

"Put down your light!" Lucas's voice came through his mask as a whisper, and only after he saw Yuri's puzzled expression did he remember that he was still transmitting through his radio. He tapped a button on his radio's controls, activating a small exterior speaker. He repeated his command and Yuri immediately complied, lowering his flashlight to point at the ground.

"Who are you? Why are you here?" Lucas barked at Yuri again as he continued to watch the hole in the ceiling and the main doorway with his thermal scope. The boy was obviously not a threat and Lucas was unsure when the mysterious shadow would reappear.

"I'm Yuri… Yuri Volkov. We just came here to explore, I swear. We're not thieves! Please don't kill me." Yuri's face was ashen and his voice trembled. Dressed in civilian clothes with a warm coat, the boy looked like a typical student who was out for an adventure. He was covered in dirt, dust and burrs and his eyes were black and tired. His entire body spoke to his exhausted and frightened state. After eyeing the boy for a moment, Lucas began to feel a measure of pity for him.

"Who else is with you, Yuri?"

Yuri paused, his gaze shifting toward the main door to the room. "My cousin, Dimitri. We came together."

Lucas glanced behind him at the door where Yuri was looking. "Where did he go?"

Yuri paused again and shook his head. "I… I don't know. He went out the door to try and talk to you, then he screamed and…"

Lucas closed his eyes and swore to himself. *Dammit!* He held up a hand at Yuri, motioning for him to stay still. "Stay here, I'll be back in just a minute. If you see that thing again, just yell for me."

Lucas walked slowly back to the entrance of the surgical theater, peeking out the door to check the hallway for any signs of the shadow. To the left, where Lucas had come from, he saw nothing on his scope except for an empty hallway. As he swung his rifle to the right he flinched, nearly pulling the trigger as the thermal scope exploded in an array of orange and yellow colors. For a second he thought the thermal signature was the shadow again, but when it didn't make any movement toward him he realized what it really was.

Coating the floor, walls and ceiling of the hallway was a thick layer of deep red blood, dripping from the ceiling tiles and pooling in small puddles on the floor. Lucas was thankful that his mask filtered out scents from the environment, though he could still imagine what the air must have smelled like. Lucas reached for his flashlight, switching it on and casting the white beam down the hall, illuminating the gory scene.

The images reminded him of Iosif's quick demise, brought about immediately after the shadow had slaughtered Yuri's companion. Lucas noticed something odd about the scene of carnage and stepped out into the hall with trepidation, keeping a wary eye behind and in front of him. *Fat lot of good that'll do when this thing can punch through walls and ceilings like they're made of paper.*

The grisly scene disturbed Lucas but he knelt down, shining his light over the spread of blood and gore across the hallway. He shook his head as he stood up, backing his way into the surgical room again. *Where's the body?* While there was an enormous amount of blood spread across the hall, Lucas was struck by the absence of any solid remains, unlike what he had seen with Iosif. If the shadow had taken this person after Iosif, then perhaps it had carried the body off to devour it. Regardless of the reasoning behind the carnage, Lucas decided that the next best course of action would be to evacuate the civilian from the hospital as quickly as possible and then return to face the threat alone.

Without Iosif's assistance, Lucas was certain that he would not be able to kill the shadow on his own, particularly since it seemed impervious to conventional weaponry. Nonetheless, he was dutybound to fulfill his mission, no matter the cost. Regardless of what it took, Lucas resolved that either he or the creature would be dead by morning.

"Yuri, get down here." Lucas spoke as loudly as he dared through his mask, not wanting to attract any more attention from the shadow. Behind him, Lucas heard the sound of footsteps running quickly down the steps, and he was soon joined by the teenager who hung behind him, nervously shining his flashlight at the door.

"I'm going to get you out of here. You need to follow me up the—"

"No way in hell. I'm not leaving."

Lucas spun, putting the tip of his SVD in Yuri's face, mere inches from his left eye. Lucas's breathing was calm and even through the mask's speaker as he spoke again. "You will leave this city. I've already lost two people tonight and I'm not losing another."

"Fuck you, soldier man, whatever your name is. I don't know who you lost, but that..." Yuri sputtered to come up with the words to describe what he had seen. "That... thing killed my cousin. Kill me now and you'll do me a favor." Yuri pushed up against the SVD, pressing his cheek against the end of the barrel. His eyes were on fire in the reflection of his flashlight, blazing with both hatred and fear as tears streamed down his cheeks. Unprepared for such a reaction, Lucas hesitated, unsure of what to do next.

After a long moment of staring at each other, Lucas finally took a step back and lowered his SVD. "If you get in my way, I'll shoot you. If you get between me and that beast, I'll shoot through you to kill it. Understand me?"

Yuri nodded and stepped around Lucas, peeking out into the hallway. His light passed back and forth, stopping on the blood that coated the walls. "My God..." Yuri whispered as he staggered into the hall, falling on his knees in front of the bloody scene. "Dimitri, you fool. Why wouldn't you listen to me."

Dimitri had been the one who encouraged them to travel to the city that night, though Yuri ultimately felt responsible for what had happened. If he had only argued more against the trip or refused to go, then Dimitri's death could have been avoided. *What am I going to say to Aunt Tamara? What am I going to say to mama?* Yuri closed his eyes and sat back on his legs, whispering an old prayer that his mother had taught him when he was just a boy. A prayer for the dead, Yuri spoke it for his cousin, begging for forgiveness both for his inaction and for Dimitri's soul.

Lucas watched Yuri from the doorway to the hall, still glancing around with his thermal scope to make sure the shadow wasn't close by. Lucas felt a twinge of pity for Yuri as the teenager sat in front of the remains of his friend, shaking his head and muttering to himself. He exited into the hallway and tapped Yuri on the back with the barrel of his SVD.

"This hospital isn't safe. We need to leave right now."

Yuri slowly stood and turned to face Lucas. The fire in his eyes hadn't lessened, but a faint reflection of what Lucas himself felt now shone through. *Vengeance for the dead*, Lucas thought, turning to lead Yuri out of the basement.

"Keep quiet unless you see the beast. Stay behind me and don't get in my way."

Yuri didn't respond to Lucas's order though he did obey, remaining quiet and walking just a few feet behind Lucas. They ascended the stairs slowly as Lucas carefully scanned his corners, checking every square inch of surface in the halls and stairs for any thermal signatures. In the cold night air, the blood on the main floor had already cooled, showing up in the thermal scope as dark blue puddles and streaks. Lucas stopped at the top of the stairs as he aimed down the hallway, bothered by something that tickled at the back of his mind.

Where's Iosif?

Chapter Seventeen
Lucas Pokrov | Yuri Volkov

In the long, dark corridor streaked with blood, Lucas realized with a start that Iosif's mangled corpse was no longer present. For a moment he thought that it had just cooled and wasn't showing up on the thermal scope, but a quick check with the flashlight showed him that this wasn't the case.

"What's wrong?" Yuri whispered behind Lucas.

"The body... it was here when I came downstairs, but it's gone now."

Yuri peeked around Lucas, closing his eyes at the scene in front of them. It was virtually identical to the one in the basement and it made Yuri sick to his stomach. Without warning he felt bile rise in his throat and he turned back to the stairs, vomiting into the stairwell. Lucas glanced back at Yuri, grimacing at what he heard. After a few dry heaves, Yuri turned back to Lucas, gulping deeply as he wiped his mouth on his jacket sleeve. He began to mutter an apology to Lucas who held up his hand, brushing off the attempt.

"Follow me and stay close."

Lucas moved forward through the blood-soaked corridor, keeping his eyes straight ahead and refusing to look up, down or to the sides. Yuri followed his lead, briefly closing his eyes as he walked, trying not to think about the squishing sounds that came from beneath his feet as he stepped through the puddles on the floor. Far ahead of him, by the main doors to the hospital, Lucas had moved swiftly forward, eager to get out of the hospital and out into the open. While the openness of the city provided its own set of challenges, Lucas was tired of being an easy target in the darkened building.

Once Lucas heard Yuri walk up behind him he turned and spoke with him. "How did you and your cousin get into the city, Yuri?"

Yuri nodded his head in the general direction of the car that he and Dimitri had brought. "We have a car, way out by the forest. We drove up from the city and parked it there, then we walked in."

Lucas shook his head. "Damn. So much for getting you out quickly."

"I already told you I'm not going. I'll die before I lose my chance to kill that thing first." Yuri leaned over and picked up a piece of a broken chair, brandishing the chair leg in his hands like a baseball bat. Lucas snorted at the sight, momentarily distracted from the seriousness of their situation by Yuri's absurdity. Lucas could see the fear etched in Yuri's face, but he was impressed by the display of bravery, no matter how foolish or hopeless it may have been. With a wry smile, Lucas held out his hand to Yuri.

"My name is Lucas Pokrov, sniper with the Spetsnaz special forces group. I'm sorry to meet you like this, Yuri, but I admire your courage."

Yuri held the chair leg in his left hand, gripping Lucas's thickly gloved hand with his right. Yuri's grip was firm, though Lucas could feel the slightest tremble in his arm. Whether this was a symptom of the cold, the youth's exhaustion or his fear, Lucas wasn't sure. He released Yuri's hand and reached up to his back, removing the shotgun that was strapped there.

"Do you know how to use one of these?" Lucas held the shotgun out for Yuri to take. Yuri's eyes went wide and he dropped the chair leg to the floor, taking the shotgun with both hands.

"Dimitri and I used to shoot sometimes." He flipped the pump-action shotgun over, examining the body of the weapon. With a rapid movement he took the pistol grip in one hand and slammed the pump back and then home again, ejecting a shell from the side of the weapon. He grinned sheepishly at Lucas and retrieved the shell, pushing it back into the gun.

Lucas nodded approvingly. "It's short range, but it packs quite a punch. Just hold on tight and don't use it unless you're right on top of the beast."

Yuri nodded and spoke again before Lucas could turn to leave. "What is that thing, Lucas? Is it some kind of bear?"

Lucas stopped mid-turn, shaking his head as he looked out the entrance of the hospital. "No, but I don't know what it is. Iosif and I dumped enough lead into it to drop a bull elephant, but it barely seemed to notice us. It's certainly no bear."

Yuri sighed as he sat down in a nearby chair, ignoring the dirt and debris that coated it. "I guess the stories about this place are true." He looked up at

Lucas, questioning him. "Why are you here, anyway? You don't look like local military."

Lucas hesitated before choosing to be open with Yuri instead of hiding his mission. "Iosif and I were sent here to kill whatever that thing is." Lucas looked behind him and backed up to a table that was pressed against the wall and leaned on it, catching his breath as he spoke. "I think Iosif had more information about it than I did. All I was told at our briefings was that it was some kind of anomaly suspected to be in the area."

Lucas looked down at his vest suddenly, sparked by a memory of Iosif. He reached into his vest pocket and pulled out the small notebook that Iosif had handed him. Lucas turned the notebook over in his hand, brushing his fingers over the deep brown leather surface. He glanced out the door of the hospital again, still concerned about the possibility of the shadow returning for them again.

"What's that?" Yuri stood up and walked closer to Lucas, holding his light up to illuminate the surface of the book. Lucas took off the rubber band that held the book closed and opened it to the first page, flipping through it to try and discern its contents.

"Looks like some kind of journal." Lucas flipped back to the first page and began reading. He skimmed the pages quickly at first, expecting to find little of interest in the small book. After the first few paragraphs, though, he began to slow down. Thoughts of the shadow that had attacked them dropped by the wayside as he read through the journal, captivated by the years-old stories told by Iosif.

Chapter Eighteen
Special Forces Field Journal
Iosif Seleznev

Feb 9, 2014
It's been just under 48 hours since we dropped in and it's all gone to hell. Krylov and Abrahamoff are the only two left. I never thought I'd have a chance to write in this damned book, but we don't have much else to do but sit here and wait to die. I'm going to outline what's happened since we dropped in and hope that a recovery team finds this one day.

Krylov and I are bruised but whole. Abrahamoff got the worst of it, losing his hand on one arm and breaking the other. I'd have him write this all out if he could, but I'm stuck transcribing what we've found out. Abrahamoff put the pieces together, figured the whole thing out. It's fucking unbelievable, but there's no other explanation for what's happened here.

Okay, Abrahamoff's telling me to start from the beginning. We dropped in 48 hours ago, under the cover of night. There were eight of us in total, six soldiers and two scientists. We three are the only ones left, two soldiers and one scientist from a group of eight that were armed to the teeth. We had enough firepower to take over a small country and we lost almost everyone.

The first few hours weren't bad. We blew a hole in the side wall of the compound and stormed in, leaving Krylov behind to watch over Abrahamoff and Gorbunov. The rest of us charged in and lit the place up. Ten minutes later and all the guards were dead, along with a few technicians who got caught in the crossfire. We rounded up the rest of the technicians and put them in a bunker, sealed them in nice and tight so we could poke around. (Abrahamoff insists that I note that we gave them food and water).

Per the mission instructions we left two men up top to guard the entrance to the main reactor while the rest of us headed down. Everything was uneventful until we hit the bottom of the elevator. There were guards left down in the reactor and they were ready for us, but we figured they'd be there. What we didn't figure on was there being three full squads. They were jammed in there, too, all spread out across the different floors.

They opened up on us when the elevator doors opened. We took out the few that were watching the elevator and got Abrahamoff and Gorbunov into a side room where we could fortify against the squads. The thing is, they weren't really concerned with us. We had a couple guys taking potshots at us, but they weren't rushing to get us or anything like that. We stayed holed up in the room for a good twenty minutes before the power gave out. That's when all hell broke loose.

Gorbunov was actually the first to go. A lot of the lights had gone out and he was standing back against the far wall of the room, separated from the rest of us. One second he was fine and the next second he was screaming and his body was torn apart. I've never seen anything like it. We thought he got shot at first until we got the lights out on the remains, or what was left of them. It was just a shitload of blood all spread out across the back of the room and a few bits of him, too. Not much else, except for this giant hole in the wall.

Right after we see what happened to Gorbunov, we start hearing screams and gunfire from the squads. They're unloading with everything. AKs, grenades, hell I think one of them must have had a rocket launcher. They were just firing wildly around the reactor, but they sure as hell didn't care. I don't know how they avoided hitting it, but they did.

It only took a few minutes for the gunfire to die down, then we were left wondering what the hell happened. Galkin volunteered to go out and see what was going on, so we sent him to do some recon. The rest of us were paranoid as shit and Abrahamoff was climbing the walls with paranoia, thinking he'd end up like Gorbunov. Just a minute after we sent Galkin out he came back, pale as a ghost. He started going on about shadows in the walls and how the squads were all dead. Before we could respond, this... thing comes out of nowhere down the hall, grabs him and snaps him in two. It was that fast, just like a twig. We were all so stunned that it got Artemiev before we could react.

We unloaded everything we had into the beast and it ran off, or that's what we thought at the time. I left Krylov with Abrahamoff in the room and ran down the hall to check everything for myself. We were trying to contact the surface team the entire time, but they had either been killed as soon as we went down or the radios couldn't penetrate through the earth. Regardless, it was pretty obvious that the three of us were on our own.

As I was coming back to the room I was met by Krylov and Abrahamoff who were running like bats out of hell, yelling about a shadow in the wall. The beast was behind them alright, just filling the hall with its mass. The three of us ran for our lives until we got here, into this room. It was just off of the main reactor with an assload of pipes and wires running directly from the reactor core into it. It looked like the best fortified room we had seen outside of the reactor itself, so we ran inside. Krylov and I turned to make a last stand against the beast, but it was unbelievable. It just stopped, right outside the room. It stood there, watching us in the dark, then it ran off and vanished.

Krylov and I were trying to figure out what happened before it came back, but it was Abrahamoff who figured it out. When we got into this room he started going ape-shit over the controls and monitors. When we eventually got him calmed down he explained that this chamber must have been what saved us. It lines up perfectly with our intel about that new weapon the Chinese were testing, the radiation bomb. Total organic destruction with minimal non-organic collateral damage. It was all here in the files, unlocked and open. I guess whoever was working on them was killed by that beast before they could close everything down.

Abrahamoff found out that this facility was built to test a radiation removal device that complemented their radiation bomb, and they set up a static field test in this room. I guess the plan was for them to detonate a nuke underground somewhere close once they got enough materials built up, then try to remove the radiation from the surrounding soil. It looks like they wanted to use the devices in tandem. They'd hit a city with a radiation bomb to kill off all the people, then they'd deploy a mobile version of this room to clean up the radiation overnight. Then they'd be able to roll in the next day and take control of the city without getting irradiated to hell.

Here's the kicker. Abrahamoff thinks this creature is some kind of radiation eating monstrosity. We poked our heads out a few times and took some readings of where it had smashed through the walls and floors and the radiation levels were off the chart. If that's true, then it explains why we're safe in here. This room is drawing power directly from the reactor so it's still cleansing the room of radiation. If that beast likes radiation, then it would think of this room as hell. I told Abrahamoff he was insane when he first suggested it, but the evidence makes sense.

Of course, there's a problem. This static device is still in the alpha stages, so it was barely working when we got in. After Abrahamoff started figuring everything out, he realized that the device was at low power and started boosting it. That's when that thing showed up again. It broke a hole through the floor of the chamber and started going wild on us. It was weakened enough by the field that we drove it back fairly quickly, but Abrahamoff took the attack the worst. He lost his hand and had his other arm broken by that thing. Krylov and I helped finish getting the power bumped up, then we tended to Abrahamoff.

Abrahamoff's asleep now. He's been drifting in and out of consciousness ever since the attack. I think he's stabilized, but there's no way we can get out of here without running into that beast again. We've been in here for over two days now and we've gotten no word from the surface team or the Chinese or anyone. We've got our emergency rations here, but I don't know how much longer we'll last before something else happens.

Abrahamoff woke up a few hours ago. He was very weak, but he started talking to us about an idea he had before he fell asleep. He thinks that if the creature is avoiding the room due to the "radiovacuum" (that's Abrahamoff's term for it, not mine) field, then if we can lure it in close and then crank the field up to maximum strength, we might be able to weaken or kill it. The problem is that we don't even know what the thing is made of, where it's from or what might interest it. Krylov thinks that it wants to kill us and that we should be the bait, but I'm not so sure about it. Abrahamoff dozed off again before we could talk to him about it so we're waiting for him to wake up again before we try anything.

I can hear the beast outside the room. I can see it sometimes, too, across the platforms. It sticks to the darkness, avoiding our lights as we try to see it. It keeps moving in to the reactor and back out again, over and over, like it's feeding. Krylov and I think that must be what it's doing, feeding on the radiation. That doesn't explain why it killed so many people, though. It could be an animal defending its territory, or perhaps it needs us for something else.

I nearly lost my gun to this strange substance we found on the ground. I think the creature must secrete it, maybe from its mouth or nose. It looks like a pile of goo on the ground, like clear gelatin or something. When you touch it, it feels that way too, for the first second. Then, it solidifies almost immediately, trapping the object that was touching it and binding it to the ground. I poked at it with the butt of my rifle and had to cut the damn thing loose. This stuff is incredibly resilient against blows, but a sharp blade renders it inert and you can just scrape it off once you've cut into it. I wonder, is this a defense mechanism, an active trapping mechanism or simply a curious byproduct of whatever this beast is?

Abrahamoff is awake again. We're going to test the device. He insists on being the bait, but Krylov and I won't allow it. He's the one who's figured out the system and he's the most important of all of us. I'm going to act as bait while he triggers the device, then we're all going to try to get out of here. May God have mercy on us if we don't make it through this.

Feb 20, 2014
Krylov is dead. So is Abrahamoff. I can't think. Can't think, can't concentrate, can barely write. I got out, with Krylov. He died within minutes, though, the poor bastard. His skin was bubbling off from the radiation. Before that thing died it got a swipe in at him, pumped him so full he was nearly glowing. The device worked, though. Killed the beast cold in its tracks. Abrahamoff distracted me, acted as bait instead. The thing got him and nailed Krylov before the device went off. I'm in a chopper, minutes from base. Have to hide this, keep it as proof to myself that this really happened. That beast disappeared, all evidence vanished. Just the blood and bodies left. At least it's dead.

Feb 23, 2019
My God, it's happening again. Five years later and it's happening again. I pray it isn't so, and I hope it isn't so, but my gut tells me otherwise. I never thought I would touch this accursed book again, but circumstances demand it. In twelve hours we leave for Ukraine, my partner and I. We are to investigate the site of the Chernobyl power plant and the nearby town of Prip'Yat. Once again I'm tasked with investigating "anomalies" in the area.

My superiors have briefed me separately from Lucas, my partner. My attempts to find out why have been met with the simple instruction to keep *him in the dark. The massacre in China is still a guarded secret, I see. Writing this information down in my field journal is a grave risk that could mean my imprisonment, but if what I fear to be true comes to fruition, we must all know what has happened.*

I have been given a small device that I am told will kill one of the beasts. It's a small cylinder containing a fuel cell and miniaturized circuitry for a portable radiovacuum. I've been instructed to use it only when I'm within a few meters of the creature, as it has a limited range and is good for only one use. The bastards are preparing me to kill a beast when they won't even tell me if one is here.

If I can confirm that another beast is present in the city, I will tell Lucas everything about it. Command can lock me away in the mines or shoot me, but it doesn't matter. No more deaths will come from this beast. I wish Abrahamoff or Krylov were still here, God rest their souls. I can't get an answer out of anyone I speak to about China. No one will talk about it for fear of being punished. Someone expected this to happen again, though, if they made the device in that room portable.

Lucas is a good kid. Tough as nails, still naïve, but a good kid. I hope this turns out to be some kind of field exercise. He doesn't need this, not if it's what I think.

Time to ride.

Chapter Nineteen
Lucas Pokrov | Yuri Volkov

Lucas turned to the last page of Iosif's field journal that contained writing. Nearly a quarter of the small book had been filled with Iosif's scribbling. Some of it was in calm, clean writing while other parts were jerky, small and rushed. While it wasn't much, Lucas finally had pieces to the puzzle that helped explain the events that had unfolded. He closed the book and stared at the leather cover, trying to wrap his mind around what he had just read.

Yuri shuffled away from him and sat back down in his chair. Both of them stared at the ground, temporarily lost in a fog of confusion after reading through the field journal together. Yuri was the first to speak after several long, quiet minutes.

"So where's the device?"

Lucas looked up at Yuri, shaking his head questioningly. "Device?"

Yuri pointed at the small book, nodding in Lucas's direction. "Yeah, from that last page. He was talking about a device that would kill the creature. So where is it?"

Lucas's mind finally started to shift back into the present. Distracted by the journal, he had momentarily forgotten where they were. With the creature still at large and no doubt still in pursuit of them, they would have to move quickly to try and kill it before it got to them again. He pushed himself up from the table, arching his shoulders and checking his SVD's magazine and safety.

"We need to check Iosif's body, or what's left of it for the device. Come on."

Lucas led Yuri back down the hall, fully on alert again for the beast. The hospital was quiet again, devoid of all sounds save for their footsteps and the wind. The scratches and rustles that heralded the arrival of the creature were nowhere to be heard, so they moved quickly, taking advantage of their time alone.

"Use your light and check for anything that looks like what he wrote down. It'll probably be silver or black."

Stepping gingerly through the blood and gore, Lucas and Yuri conducted a hasty examination of the hallway where Iosif had been killed. Moments passed in silence as they checked the full length of the hall, with Lucas going so far as to look in the hole the beast had created when it broke through to slaughter his partner.

"Nothing. Damn!" Lucas kicked the wall in anger, sending a thud reverberating through the wall.

Yuri looked over at him. "I'm not seeing much of anything, actually."

While the floor, walls and ceiling of the hallway had been coated with blood and a small amount of flesh, the majority of what constituted an average body was nowhere to be found. Clothing, limbs and even Iosif's equipment – including his gun – weren't anywhere in the hallway. Lucas stopped his mumbled ranting and pondered the fact before turning to face Yuri.

"Okay, so he's not here. Did that thing eat him?"

Yuri shook his head. "How would I know? His body's not here, and neither was Dimitri's. Either that thing's eating them or carrying them off somewhere."

Lucas nodded slowly and turned to head out the front door of the hospital. "Come on, I have an idea."

As the pair exited the hospital entrance, a brisk wind caused Yuri to shiver involuntarily. He pulled his jacket tighter around his body, clutching the shotgun tight against his chest. The dark silence of the city felt more ominous than ever before, thanks to the revelation of the creature that was now actively hunting them. Yuri kept close to Lucas's side, hanging back only a few feet to keep from bumping into him or his rifle. Lucas had his SVD at the ready, occasionally stopping and kneeling down in the grass to look at the area with the SVD's thermal and night vision scopes.

As they walked, Lucas held his Geiger counter in his left hand, waving it about as he let it guide them around the city. A half hour passed in silence, aside from the frantic ticking of the radiation meter. Finally, as they paused again for Lucas to do thermal and infrared scans, Yuri crouched next to him and whispered.

"Where are we going?"

Lucas didn't stop his scans as he replied to Yuri, his hushed tone nearly drowned out by the background static of his mask's speaker. "The way I figure it, this thing is so overloaded with radiation that it's got to be releasing it from time to time. Maybe not everywhere it goes, but enough that it leaves certain clues to where it's been. We're following the biggest hotspots of radiation around the city, trying to trail this thing back to where it spends the most time. Hopefully that, wherever it is, is the thing's home. If we can find its home, maybe we can find what's left of Iosif."

"What about the radiation? Won't it harm us?"

"No, the masks will keep us – oh. Right." Lucas glanced at Yuri quickly, looking him up and down. He turned the Geiger counter on Yuri, giving him a quick scan. "You look pretty clean. Just don't rub your hands in the hotspots and stick your fingers in your mouth and you should be okay. The hotspots I'm seeing so far are very condensed, so as long as you keep your distance you'll be fine."

Yuri gulped nervously, rubbing his hands on his jacket in a vain attempt to remove the radiation he was now certain was coating them. Lucas stood again and continued walking forward, and Yuri hurried to catch up. They continued to weave their way through the city's depths, stopping to check for radiation, backtracking along false trails and checking any buildings in their path. The utter stillness of the city was unnerving to Yuri, particularly since he and Dimitri had spent much of their time fleeing from their pursuer. The moon was past its apex now, slowly making its way down through the sky. Yuri was glad that daylight would soon be on its way, though it was only just past one in the morning. With several hours of darkness left, Lucas and Yuri had to remain vigilant against the shadow lurking in the city.

After an hour of wandering through buildings and fields, Lucas and Yuri came to an open area in between the city of Prip'Yat and the Chernobyl power plant. Located just over a mile from Prip'Yat, the power plant was clearly illuminated against the night sky by the moon. Lucas walked past the main road out of the city, sweeping the Geiger counter back and forth. He stopped after a moment and motioned for Yuri to come close to him.

"Tell me something. If this thing loves radiation and leaves trails of it behind as it walks, what would be the best place to get all the radiation it wants at the same time as it hides its trail?"

Yuri looked to where Lucas was staring, beyond the field and construction equipment in the distance to the sarcophagus and chimney in the distance. Built in the months after the disaster, the sarcophagus was designed to keep the radiation from the disaster contained. Together with the red and white chimney, the sarcophagus was another iconic image of Chernobyl, recognizable to anyone with even a passing familiarity of the disaster.

Although the construction of the sarcophagus had helped to slow the leakage of radiation, the area surrounding the power plant still contained lethal doses, enough to fatally irradiate a man if he made even a single misstep. The radiation levels at the power plant were much greater than the radiation left behind by the beast, providing the perfect cover for a creature that thrived in such an environment.

"Can't you call in backup?"

Lucas shook his head as he checked his rifle and gear again, preparing for the long walk to the station. "No. They wouldn't send anyone even if I contacted them. This is a black op. Only the most senior officials in Ukraine even know we're here. To send in any more troops or to call in reinforcements from Ukraine would generate questions that nobody wants to answer."

Yuri started to speak but couldn't find the words to express what he felt. Traveling to the power station would mean almost certain death, but if they wanted to find the beast that had killed their comrades, it was the only choice left open to them.

Chapter Twenty
Chernobyl Nuclear Power Plant
Reactor Number Four

Water drips from the ceiling of the mighty sarcophagus, cascading down into the dirt and concrete below. Perpetual puddles form small rivers inside the remains of reactor number four, winding their way through the rebar and reinforced steel structure that was torn apart by the destruction in 1986. Inside the sarcophagus the air is still thick and stale. Though circulation was once assisted by blowers, they have been neglected over the years, left to fall apart due to the lack of funding and manpower required to repair them.

The scent of rotting meat is strong inside the chamber. Strips of flesh, piles of bones and scattered remains of clothing, weapons and other gear are strewn in piles, adding to the bleak and gruesome atmosphere. Skulls that were gnawed clean months ago sit next to ones still covered in skin and muscle. Decapitated bodies lay in various positions, all in different states of decay and dismemberment. No light shines through, even in full daylight, thanks to the thick concrete walls of the sarcophagus. Time and nature have had their way, though, forming small holes and crevices through which spores, seeds, water and other things have infiltrated the structure.

Through this toxic maze of concrete, flesh, bone and radiation, a shadow walks. Darker than the blackness inside the sarcophagus, it moves slowly around corners and through passageways, winding its way along a familiar path from the exterior of the chamber into the very center. The beast's bulky body is enormous, taller than a grizzly bear and as wide as an elephant. The beast makes little sound as it moves, only a slight rustle as it passes around obstacles in its path. The sheer size of the creature contrasts starkly with its movement as it behaves more like a liquid than a living being. Its body seems to shrink as it passes through narrow spaces in walkways and under fallen walls, treading a slow and steady path to the heart of the remains of the nuclear reactor itself.

Covered in a thick, short fur, the beast's eyes are sunken into its skull, protecting them from attacks by sacrificing peripheral vision. It walks on four powerful legs that each bristle with fearsome claws, most of which have been stained red. Large ears twitch at the sides of the beasts head as it walks along, paying attention for any signs of danger in its inner sanctum. The beast's nose runs with moisture that drips to the ground, forming small clear blobs that stick to the floor. Beneath the nose, just at the end of a short snout, the beast's mouth is closed, though the ends of razor-sharp teeth are still visible. Bits of bone and cloth hang from the creature's teeth, remnants of its previous kills.

As the creature passes into the center of the sarcophagus, it brushes past the steel beams that lay strewn about, shuddering in pleasure as it absorbs massive amounts of radiation into its body. The largest of these beams sits nearly vertical in the ground, having been lodged there from the room of the structure during the initial explosion. Here, at ground zero of the disaster, the radiation levels are off the chart, promising certain death to nearly any living thing that might try to venture this deep into the facility.

The beast is not put off by the radiation. On the contrary, it actively seeks it out. At the base of the beam is a nesting area where a portion of ground has been flattened and smoothed out into a resting place. Satiated after its meal, the beast curls its body around the beam, preparing to slumber and rest after a long night of hunting. The glow of the beast's red eyes gradually fades away to nothing as it falls asleep, its chest gently rising and falling in time with its slow breathing.

Food.

The slumbering form of the beast twitches as its sensitive nose picks up on the scent of fresh game. Its red eyes open into small slits as it awakens. The beast is driven ever forward by the pursuit of sustenance, though the smell of fresh meat is not the only odor in the air. Now fully awake, the beast holds its head high, picking out traces of other scents, too. Fear, determination and anxiety mingle with lead and explosives. The creature snarls at this scent, revealing rows of teeth. A long scar stretches down the side of its face, freshly made from its most recent encounter. Though it has faced opposition in the past, a single piece of game has never put up such a fierce resistance as the one earlier in the night. The damage to the creature was minimal but it remains on guard.

Chapter Twenty-One
Lucas Pokrov | Yuri Volkov

"Walk only where I walk. If you don't stay in my footsteps, you'll wish for a quick death."

Lucas's warning was well heeded by Yuri, who used his flashlight to carefully ensure that he trod only where Lucas had stepped. While Lucas was somewhat protected from the massive hotspots of radiation around the power plant thanks to his specialized suit and mask, Yuri was not so fortunate. With a pair of hiking boots and civilian clothing, he would have no opportunity to save himself from a radiation hotspot should he inadvertently stumble into one.

It had taken Yuri and Lucas just over an hour to make their way to the power plant. In addition to passing through fields and small stands of trees, they had to contend with more unpleasant obstacles, such as the neglected oil storage facility and pits filled with radioactive sand and soil. Lucas was vigilant with his radiation meter, scanning both the ground ahead of them as well as Yuri's body. Lucas was certain they were on the correct path as he continued to detect random intense hotspots of radiation along their path. Though they certainly could have occurred as a result of the disaster, the direction they lay in pointed directly toward the power plant, which – in Lucas's mind – was not a coincidence.

The power plant's outer perimeter was just as quiet as the city, though the wind was louder here, having picked up slightly since they left the protection of the tall buildings. Yuri's hands were chilled and his lips chapped from the cold, but he still clung to the shotgun, fighting to keep from shivering as he kept it up and pointed ahead of them. Now that they were within the outer boundary of the power plant, Yuri could make out more details of the plant itself.

Although the original sarcophagus over the plant was still standing, the newer one was not. The first sarcophagus had been built hastily and was only supposed to remain in place for twenty years. A new, more sophisticated one was designed, called the New Safe Confinement. Scheduled to be finished in 2015, the containment structure suffered a series of unfortunate accidents, resulting in the complete dismantlement of the portions that were already built. A complete suspension of the project was put into place due to a lack of funding, and a small amount of money was thrown at the original containment structure to help keep it in place until a new one could be built.

Due to the fact that the sarcophagus was built in part on top of the damaged power plant, it was never entirely stable, a fact that was not lost on the residents in nearby cities and countries. Worsening international tensions decreased attention and funding to the problem and local authorities quietly slipped into a reactionary mode. While they did keep a close eye on the structure, they also put little additional work into repairing it unless serious problems developed.

The remnants of the new containment unit construction yard were breathtaking to Yuri, who had never seen anything like it before. Curved pieces of steel and concrete towered into the air, joined together into unfinished half arches that were to be lined up and slid over the existing structure. Massive cranes and earth moving equipment were still present as well, more victims of the shutdown of construction on the containment structure.

At the edge of one of the half-arches, Lucas paused and looked upward at the great piece of steel. He passed his Geiger counter to Yuri and put a foot up on the arch. "Keep this on. If it starts going wild, yell like you mean it and then get up here with me. I'm going to take a quick look from up there and see if I can spot anywhere nearby where this thing might have gone."

High up on the steel structure, Lucas felt the cold of the metal bleeding through his gloves to sting his hands. He climbed slowly to the peak of the half-arch and sat down, keeping his legs and feet tight against the surface to prevent himself from slipping. He slowly maneuvered his SVD from his back and raised it up, switching from his night vision scope to his thermal one. Since they were just a few thousand feet from the walls of the sarcophagus that covered the power plant, Lucas scanned the area slowly, looking for signs of thermal activity. Various portions of the building and surrounding land appeared slightly warmer or colder based on how much heat they had retained from the day, but overall there was no sign of anything significant that stood out.

Switching to his night vision scope, Lucas continued scanning the area, focusing his efforts on the sarcophagus and the main chimney. He flinched as he caught movement near the top of the chimney, putting one hand out to balance himself and keep from falling off. At the top of the red and white tower, a dark shape emerged, showing up as pure black on the scope. Large limbs pulled the beast up and over the edge of the tower, then it slowly descended, leaping across support beams as it descended the structure.

When the creature had reached the halfway point on the chimney, it stopped and lifted its head as though it was smelling the wind. As the beast turned its head toward Lucas it stopped, its glowing eyes shining brightly in his night vision scope. Lucas felt a chill run down his spine as the creature stared at him, its head cocked slightly to the side. He could swear that it was studying him, though he dismissed the thought. *It can't see me from that far away,* he thought.

The beast snarled and gave one last look in Lucas's direction before finishing its descent down the chimney, where it quickly disappeared into the structures around the power plant. Lucas continued to watch the area for a few moments, searching for any sight of the creature, but finally gave up when no more movement was present.

After slinging the SVD on his back again, Lucas made a hurried descent of his own down the side of the half arch, half climbing and half sliding until he reached the bottom. He immediately pulled his SVD back out and dropped low into a crouch, scanning the area around himself and Yuri.

"What happened? Did you see anything?" Yuri's voice shook with cold and fright as he stood next to Lucas.

"We found the right place, but I think that thing found us, too."

Chapter Twenty-Two
Lucas Pokrov | Yuri Volkov

"It knows we're here? Shit!" Yuri began to pace the ground next to Lucas, talking loudly to himself as he began to panic.

"Shut up and get over here now!" Lucas hissed at Yuri, startling him but causing him to obey the instructions. Yuri knelt down on the ground next to Lucas who still kept guard, scanning the area around them with his thermal and night vision scopes. Yuri whispered to Lucas, fighting to keep his voice calm as he spoke.

"Sorry. What do we do now?"

Lucas didn't look away from his scope as he held the SVD in his right hand. He used his left hand to fish a small device out of his vest pouch and handed it to Yuri.

"Flip the switch on the end and then push the red button on this. If the transmitter inside Iosif's suit is still intact, it'll activate and start transmitting his location."

"What?" Yuri was shocked at this revelation and nearly dropped the device in shock. "Why didn't we do this before?"

Lucas grimaced as he spoke. "You'll see. Just push it."

Yuri turned the device over in his hands, examining its surface. It was slightly larger than a lighter and had three raised buttons on its surface along with a small power switch at one end. Yuri slid the switch to the on position, causing the three buttons to glow their respective colors: red, green and blue. Yuri flinched as he depressed the red button, half-expecting the device to shock him or jump out of his hand.

For a few seconds, nothing happened, and Yuri thought that the button had done nothing. Then, from the depths of the power plant, a sound echoed forth. It pulsed in a high-pitched tone, sounding like an alarm clock on steroids. Yuri looked at Lucas as he took back the small device.

"What is that?"

"Audible transponder. All the radiation around here makes it impossible to track Iosif's suit through any other means, so what you just switched on is that last-ditch emergency audible transponder located in his gear. I didn't want to activate it until I was certain we were close by since we're not the only ones who can follow it."

Lucas stood and moved forward quickly through the construction area, heading toward the western cooling lake to the south of the power plant. Though it was difficult to tell exactly where the sound was coming from, both Yuri and Lucas agreed that it was roughly in the direction of the power plant, the same place that Lucas had spotted the creature.

Knowing that they were treading on the territory of the beast, Yuri forgot his cold and chills and focused on following Lucas as closely as possible. As Lucas scanned ahead of them, Yuri kept his eye behind them, watching on the ground and up in buildings and other structures for any signs of the shadowy creature. Although Yuri only held a simple shotgun for protection, he put his full confidence in Lucas who had already chased the creature off once before.

The alarm grew louder as the pair drew closer toward the western cooling lake. The lakes were once used as reservoirs for cooling the power plant, but were drained shortly after the disaster. Constructed of concrete, they had quickly seen growth of plants and algae that were fed by the rainwater that fell into the lake. This plant material absorbed a large amount of radiation, which in turn caused the lakes to develop hotspots over the years. This, plus their close proximity to the nuclear power plant, made them a dangerous place to visit since one wrong slip could mean tumbling down into a pit of radiation.

On the southern side of the sarcophagus Lucas and Yuri could see the abandoned remains of reactor buildings one, two and three stretching eastward from the sarcophagus covering reactor number four. These reactors were kept online for years after the disaster, culminating in shutdowns in the 1990's and a total decommission in 2000. Plans were made to spend the next two decades removing the radioactive waste from at a slow and calculated pace. After the Ukrainian government began to encounter financial difficulties, though, they sold the fuel to China at a reduced rate with the agreement that everything would be removed by

2016. This led to a complete abandonment of the site, and all personnel who still worked at the power plant were reassigned or quietly retired.

Standing at the edge of the cooling lake, Lucas looked around with his scopes. Satisfied that – for the moment – they were alone, he switched on his flashlight, illuminating the empty concrete lake in front of them, in search of the alarm that sounded like it was right next to them. Yuri clapped his hand over his mouth to stifle a yelp as the contents of the lake bed were revealed.

Bones, tattered clothing, backpacks and even a few guns were scattered in the pit, spread out over its length in a thin layer. Hidden in the dark and masked by the cold, both the sight and smell of the contents of the lake bed had been obscured from the pair during their approach. Even during the daylight, from any farther than a hundred feet away, the brush and grasses growing in the defunct lake camouflaged its contents from observers.

Yuri shook his head in disbelief. "How is this even possible? There must be dozens of bodies down there. How has no one discovered this?"

Lucas began to walk along the perimeter, searching for an easy way down as he spoke. "This part of the complex is pretty isolated. No one would normally come down here due to the radiation. The closest visitors get to the sarcophagus is the center north of what used to be the new sarcophagus construction yard. Plus, there's no clear line of sight to the lake bed from the roads. Aside from stashing these remains inside a building, there's no better place to do it."

"Why go to all this trouble?" Yuri followed close behind Lucas, following him down the easiest slope into the lake bed. The sound of the transponder was close now, within a few dozen feet.

"Who knows. Maybe after it cleans the bodies of anything edible it deposits them here? I guess it could be marking its territory, or hell, this could even be its nest, though it seems too open for that."

The mere suggestion that they could be walking in the beast's very lair made Yuri's heart race. He felt his chest constrict with panic and tried to force himself to calm down. Lucas had slowed again after taking back his Geiger counter from Yuri and was again scanning their path, stopping every few feet to check for radiation hotspots. He led them on a winding path through the lake bed, slowly picking his way toward a cluster of garments and gear near the edge of the lake opposite where they had entered.

"It's getting hot up ahead. You stay here, I'll go on. I'll be fine for a few minutes in this mess." Yuri nodded and crouched down, keeping on the lookout for the beast. The high-pitched alarm was beginning to give him a headache, and he wondered how much longer it would be before the creature became curious enough about the foreign noise to come and investigate it.

Moving on ahead, Lucas quickly moved over the piles of discarded remains, trying not to think about the massive amounts of radiation that he was more than likely exposing himself to. As he grew close to the source of the alarm, he pulled out the activation device from his vest and depressed the red button again, silencing the alarm. He then pressed the blue button on the device. A few seconds later, a soft glow emanated from beneath a pile of blood-soaked clothing. The material was still moist and Lucas was grateful for his suit's gloves as he pulled aside the cloth, exposing what was left of Iosif's gear.

Iosif's vest was nearly intact, aside from being shredded in half. Blood had soaked entirely through it, turning the black fabric a shade of deep crimson in the glow of Lucas's flashlight. He quickly searched through the pockets of the vest, finally coming upon what he had been searching for. Inside the lower back pocket, a cylinder the size of a soda can was nestled inside a small bag along with a device similar to the one he had used to locate the gear. While the cylinder itself appeared intact, the remote control hadn't fared as well, having been sliced open on one end by the creature's fearsome claws.

Why the hell would it need a remote, anyway? Lucas mused over this new piece of the puzzle before he tucked the bag containing the damaged remote and the intact cylinder into a pocket on his vest. He turned around, preparing to head back to Yuri, when movement on the ridge of the cooling lake caught his eye. Lucas pulled his SVD up, aiming it in the direction of the movement and stared down the scope.

In the inky blackness, slinking along nearly out of view, a pair of glowing eyes appeared in the night vision scope, accompanied by the familiar black mass attached to them. Lucas kept still as he watched the creature pace slowly

85

along, watching the pair who were crouched in the cooling lake. Lucas silently prayed that Yuri would not notice the presence of the creature and make any sudden moves, but this hope was short-lived.

Out of the corner of his other eye, Lucas saw Yuri turn to look in the direction the SVD was pointing. A few seconds passed in silence as Yuri processed the sight of the creature on the edge of the lake. As recognition dawned over what it was, he let out a scream and raised his shotgun, preparing to fire on the beast.

"No! Don't shoot!" Lucas called to Yuri and started to run toward him, trying to close the gap between himself and the young man. His cry of warning came a few seconds too late, though, as Yuri began to fire at the beast with the shotgun. Enraged, the beast ducked out of sight for a moment, disappearing from Lucas's scope as Yuri continued to fire wildly into the darkness.

Lucas grabbed Yuri's arm, pulling him along as he ran, trying to keep an eye on both where they were running and where he last saw the creature at the same time. Yuri stumbled along behind Lucas, having dropped his shotgun in the confusion.

"Get up the slope, quick!" Lucas yelled at Yuri, all pretense of stealth having been abandoned. Lucas pushed Yuri up ahead of him, holding his SVD scope up to his eye to try and catch sight of the creature. In all of the jostling, Lucas finally saw what he was looking for. On the opposite side of the cooling lake, the massive form of the beast tore along the rim of the lake, heading directly for them. With Yuri and Lucas both now out of the pit, there were only a few seconds left to make a decision about what to do next before the creature would be upon them.

Oddly enough, Yuri was the first one to make a move. He began to run across the nearby field, heading for the reactor buildings in the distance. Lucas ran after him, struggling to keep up with Yuri's sudden burst of energy.

"Just ahead, do you see it?" Yuri yelled back to Lucas who was only a few paces behind. In front of them, a small structure stood in the middle of the field. No larger than an outhouse, it was painted white and had a single steel door that led inside. Lucas immediately recognized it as an underground bunker entrance and realized what Yuri was doing.

86

While going underground would in no way guarantee that they would be able to lose the creature, Lucas couldn't think of any other alternatives that were close enough. As they reached the door, Yuri pulled the handle, overjoyed to find that it was unlocked. He flung the door open and stepped inside, facing a large hatch with an oversized wheel on the ground inside the structure.

Lucas slid to a stop behind Yuri just in front of the structure and brought his SVD up in a ready position, preparing to fire on the creature. "Open the hatch! I'll cover you!" Yuri knelt down and frantically began to turn the rusty wheel. Though the old metal whined and groaned in protest at first, it gradually gave way and the wheel spun freely, unlocking the hatch. With a grunt, Yuri lifted the hatch and began his descent down the ladder, vanishing quickly into the darkness.

Lucas continued to back up into the structure, having lost sight of the creature during their brief run. Hesitating for a moment, he quickly turned around and descended the ladder, slinging his SVD over his shoulder. After he was a few feet down the ladder he pulled on the steel hatch, swinging it slowly over until its weight brought it down with a loud bang. As he began to turn the wheel on the hatch, a powerful thud came from the other side that caused the wheel to bend inward, striking him on the arm. Lucas hurried down the ladder after Yuri as the pounding on the hatch increased, accompanied by angry snarls as the beast tried to break through the thick steel barrier to pursue its prey.

Chapter Twenty-Three
Lucas Pokrov | Yuri Volkov

Lucas jumped the last few feet off the ladder, landing with a grunt next to Yuri. Wide eyed and shaking, Yuri whispered to Lucas. "Are you okay?"

Lucas nodded and held a finger up in front of his face, indicating that Yuri should remain silent. From the shaft above them the relentless pounding continued, though the hatch still showed no signs of yielding under the onslaught. Lucas turned his flashlight on and scanned it around the tunnel, trying to get some idea of where they were.

The underground area was damp and cramped. The small chamber they were both squatting in was barely tall enough for them to stand and it stretched off in three directions through narrow tunnels. Antiquated pipes and wiring lined the walls of the tunnels, leaving little room for someone to traverse them. Though Lucas couldn't get a sense of the smell of the place due to his mask, Yuri wrinkled his nose at the musty odors that permeated the underground tunnels.

The construction of the place was a collection of brick, concrete blocks, steel support beams and rotting wooden walkways that extended over deep caverns. Lucas and Yuri both knew little of the underground complex, though each had their own perspective on the area. Yuri had grown up hearing whispers of the underground as a place where "mole people" lived, blinded by the radiation and reduced to scrounging for rats and insects for food. Lucas recalled that the underground had been mentioned in one of his briefings, but couldn't remember any specifics about it.

The tunnel system extended throughout the lower portions of Chernobyl, linking the various buildings to each other. Their primary purpose was for steam transportation, ventilation, piping and wiring, but they were also used as a more convenient way to travel around the plant during the winter, when the snowfall could be measured in feet. The unofficial nature of this use meant that they weren't maintained as well as might otherwise be expected, so the years of neglect had been less kind to the tunnel system than it had to other areas of the power plant complex.

Lucas checked a compass embedded in the stock of his SVD and pointed down the tunnel that branched off to their right. Yuri followed Lucas down the tunnel as they half crouched and half ran, moving away from the entrance as quickly as possible. After several minutes of walking they could no longer hear the pounding from the creature and they stopped in a small alcove to rest. Lucas confirmed that the radiation level in the tunnel was not dangerous and Yuri plopped down on the floor, glad to be off of his feet.

Lucas sat down across from Yuri and retrieved the cylinder from his vest. He pulled it out of its bag along with the damaged remote control and began to examine them. Yuri watched as Lucas turned the cylinder over, trying to figure out how it worked. The cylinder was matte black in color with two distinct halves separated by a half-inch strip of silver metal. Two indentations sat at either end of the cylinder and appeared to have lights in them, though neither indent was glowing at the moment.

"This looks like one of the new stun grenades," Lucas mumbled, "but the size is all wrong. This is at least five times as large."

Yuri interrupted Lucas's examination of the object. "Is that the thing that'll kill the creature?"

Lucas nodded slowly in response. "I think so. I'm not completely sure, but I think it will. It looks like what Iosif described, but I'll have to figure out how to detonate it."

Lucas continued to turn the device in his hand as he spoke and inadvertently slipped one of his fingers onto an indent at the end of the cylinder. The two halves immediately popped apart, lengthening the device by a full six inches and revealing a small panel and keyboard in the center of the device. The screen bloomed to life and Yuri scooted around to view it alongside Lucas.

After a series of flashing lines passed by as the device performed a status check. Each line ended with a small green dot indicating that the device's systems were functioning properly. The last line, however, was different. Instead of a green dot, a flashing red "x" was present after the words "Remote detonation control status." Lucas looked at the broken remote control where he had placed it on the ground and closed his eyes in frustration.

"Damn. We can't set this thing off remotely."

"Who cares?" Yuri picked up the remote and looked it over before throwing it back on the floor. "It just removes radiation, right? It shouldn't hurt us, just that creature."

Lucas shook his head and turned the cylinder around for Yuri to get a clearer view of the status panel. "Look at these two lines."

Yuri squinted at the small screen, reading the lines that Lucas was pointing to.

Radiovacuum status ----- Ready.
High explosives status ----- Ready.

"Wait, high explosives?" Yuri backed away from Lucas as he nervously stared at the cylinder. "I thought this thing just removed radiation from an environment!"

"It looks like there were some upgrades to the original design. I guess whoever made this didn't want to take any chances at killing one of these creatures. There's enough explosive material in here to level a city block." Lucas poked at the keyboard on the device, watching as the screen changed to show schematics of the device, along with simple instructions for arming and detonating it both remotely and locally.

Satisfied that he knew how to operate the device, Lucas closed it and returned it to the pocket on his vest. He looked at Yuri who was slowly nodding his head. Yuri looked up and met Lucas's eyes through the face mask, then he spoke with the defeated tone of a man resigned to his fate.

"Okay. Let's do it. Let's kill this bastard."

Lucas stood up and held out his hand to Yuri. The youth grabbed the proffered hand and stood, staring at Lucas as the soldier spoke to him. "You can still leave, you know. You're a civilian and you aren't supposed to be here. Just hide in the tunnels until the thing's dead, then you can get back to your car before the recovery team comes to pick me up."

"Even if I wanted to do that, what would I tell my family and friends? How am I supposed to explain to my aunt that her son died? I let him go out there alone and this thing killed him, but I'm not letting it end like that." Yuri shook his head and gritted his teeth as anger rose in his voice. "No. Like it or not, I'm coming with you. This thing scares the hell out of me, but it killed my best friend. There's no way I'm running away from it."

Lucas sighed deeply and patted Yuri on the back. He briefly considered trying to force Yuri to do as he suggested, but he knew that would be an impossible battle. Despite the dangers, Yuri was dead set on avenging the death of his comrade, a feeling that Lucas knew too well.

"Come on, then. Let's get going."

Chapter Twenty-Four
Lucas Pokrov | Yuri Volkov

Time passed by slowly underground. While it felt like they had been traveling for hours, every time Yuri glanced at his watch he was surprised that less than a half hour had passed. Ducking around corners, slinking down corridors and leaping over crevices in the tunnels had left Yuri wondering where they were in the complex. Lucas appeared to know exactly where he was going though as he deftly maneuvered them around collapsed sections of the tunnels, through abandoned maintenance bays and even through a few surface level buildings.

Ever since leaving the creature behind at the hatch, neither Lucas nor Yuri had seen nor heard any sign of the beast. Yuri decided that if it had left them alone for this long then it must not have been able to find where they were. While this was somewhat unsurprising given the seeming randomness of their trek, he still felt some unease about the assumption that the creature wouldn't know the area around its own home well enough to find them. Regardless of the true reasons behind being left alone by the beast, Yuri was glad for the temporary reprieve, especially after the close call near the cooling lakes.

Lost in his thoughts, Yuri bumped into the back of Lucas as the soldier abruptly stopped at an intersection. Yuri backed up as Lucas pulled out his Geiger counter and went from tunnel to tunnel, measuring the radioactivity in each passageway. With a satisfied grunt he put the Geiger counter away and turned back to Yuri.

"I think we're close to its lair. I've been trying to follow the radiation trail to find a passage that leads near the main reactor chamber and I think this is it. The measurements from that tunnel are rising abnormally fast, probably from water runoff in the soil."

Yuri nodded. "What's to wait around for? Let's get in there and kill it!" He started to walk down the passageway, but Lucas held up his arm, blocking Yuri's path.

"Yuri, you can't go down there. The radiation levels are going to get much, much higher. Even if that thing doesn't get you, if you go anywhere near the reactor chamber, you'll die anyway."

Yuri frowned at Lucas and stood his ground, refusing to be pushed back. "If you go in, I go in."

"I don't have time to argue about this, Yuri." Lucas drew his SVD and stepped back, raising it to aim at Yuri. "I'm sorry about your cousin, but I'm not going to let you—"

A crash from above the pair stopped Lucas mid-sentence. Both Yuri and Lucas stepped back into the tunnel they had come from. They shone their lights down the other tunnels of the intersection, trying to find the source of the sound. Lucas's thermal and night vision scopes showed no evidence of anything in the passages, but the sound had most definitely been close by.

After several seconds of silence, Yuri was preparing to speak, thinking that the noise was just something in a building overhead that had been knocked over by the wind. He opened his mouth to talk, but a second crash, this time much closer, made him snap his jaw shut. Lucas leaned his head out of the tunnel, glancing upward in the intersection.

Most of the passageway intersections had tall roofs and the remains of ladders that had once gone from the bottom of the intersection up to the top, where more hatches were no doubt positioned. All of the intersections that Yuri and Lucas had passed had no usable ladders, though, so they dismissed the intersections as mere curiosities, not realizing that the beast was using them to track his prey. Once they had reached an intersection with a weakened hatch, the beast struck, pounding away at the hatch with such ferocity that he had nearly torn it off with just two blows.

A third impact came several seconds later, though this one was accompanied by the sound of rushing air and the clatter of broken bolts as they rained down into the intersection from the smashed hatch. Lucas pushed Yuri into a side tunnel, directing them away from the passage to the reactor chamber. Yuri stumbled ahead as snarls came from the behind them, accompanied by the familiar rustle and clatter of the beast's body and claws as it descended into the tunnels.

Instead of dropping directly to the ground, the beast had its claws dug firmly into the concrete walls of the intersection, crawling swiftly downward in a manner reminiscent of a reptile. The face of the beast appeared at the top of the tunnel entrance as Lucas backed up, retreating behind Yuri. Rows of teeth were revealed as the beast snarled openly at Lucas, who responded by raising his rifle toward the creature.

Remembering their last encounter, the beast quickly tucked its head out of the way as Lucas fired off two shots, both of which missed their target and impacted on the opposite wall. The powerful rounds exploded upon impact, showering the intersection with fragments of metal and concrete and causing the beast to lose its footing. The dark shape of the creature fell to the ground in a heap, though it was swiftly back on its feet. In the infrared scope of his SVD, Lucas watched the creature back up out of the tunnel to hide just out of sight.

"Keep moving!" Lucas called back to Yuri, whose only response was a grunt as he continued running down the passage. After several more minutes of running, Yuri and Lucas slowed again and strained to listen for the creature. Silence was their only companion, though, which once again proved to be more unnerving than knowing where the beast was. Stuck in a long stretch of winding tunnel with no nearby intersections or ways of escape, Lucas took up the lead and left Yuri to watch their backs with his flashlight.

Lucas stopped every few seconds to check his compass, trying to get an idea of where they were. He cursed hoarsely, still struggling to get enough air through his mask. "Shit! I have no idea where we are."

Yuri started to reply when a slight vibration in the air gave him pause. He cocked his head and pointed upward to the low ceiling as he tapped Lucas on the shoulder. Lucas nodded in confirmation that he had heard the sound as well, then quietly began to retreat back down the hallway in the direction they had come from. A few feet ahead, where they had just been standing, the vibrations became worse and pieces of the ceiling began to shatter and fall to the ground.

"Go!" Lucas shouted at Yuri, who turned and ran back down the hall. As he ran, the ceiling in front of Lucas finally caved in and a shadowy mass dropped into the hallway. In his thermal scope, Lucas couldn't make out any details of the mass, but his night vision scope clearly showed the creature's outline, along with its two red, glowing eyes.

The beast snarled at Lucas and began to charge down the hall, gaining speed at a frightening rate. Lucas backed down the hall as quickly as he could, keeping the SVD trained on the creature. Only when the shadow had come within twenty feet of Lucas did he open fire, squeezing off two quick rounds from the SVD in rapid succession. The rounds exploded against the beast's body, lighting up the hallway with brief flashes, though they didn't seem to cause any ill effects to the creature itself.

Lucas could hear Yuri behind him, still running through the tunnel, then stopping as he reached what Yuri assumed to be the intersection. He continued to fire at the creature, which other than causing it to snarl and slow down slightly, was still having no effect. *Damn! Did this thing grow body armor or something?*

With only five rounds left in his current magazine and no time left to swap in another one, Lucas decided that it was time to put his sniper training to good use. He raised the rifle a few inches, leveling it with the creature's face. Dropping to one knee, he pressed the rifle deep into his shoulder and flipped both scopes down. Lucas stared down the iron sights of the SVD and squeezed the trigger rapidly, dropping four rounds into the creature's right eye socket. Lucas's motions were so quick that the beast had barely gained any ground and was still several feet away when the explosives from the rounds went off.

Even from underneath his protective mask, Lucas's ears still rang from the concussive blasts of the rounds. These were accompanied by a loud howling groan from the creature as it skidded to a stop. With one round left, Lucas dropped it into the center of the creature's face where he assumed its nose or mouth might be. While the previous shots had startled, wounded and enraged the beast, the fifth shot was the last straw for the creature. Viscous liquid was expelled from the creature's face from the impact, a mixture of the clear gelatin-like substance and a dark, black substance that Lucas had never seen before. The beast backpedalled down the passage, leaving Lucas to watch it retreat, panting heavily as he saw the single red eye vanish around a corner.

A moment of silence passed as Lucas kept watch down the hall, having quickly swapped out the empty magazine in his SVD for a full one. He wiped the strange substances from his chest and mask, puzzled by the dark liquid yet glad that there wasn't enough of the clear gelatin on him to harden and cause damage to his gear. Yuri's quiet footsteps sounded from behind him and he turned his head to check on him.

"You alright?"

"Yeah, I'm fine. How about you? That was one hell of a loud firefight."

Lucas smirked and stood, satisfied that they were safe for the moment. "Fine here. That thing's not, though. I think I took out one of its eyes."

Yuri grinned broadly as he congratulated Lucas. "Hot damn! That's fantastic!"

"Maybe." Lucas shrugged. "I didn't kill it, and now it's wounded. If that thing's like any other wild animal, all I did was piss it off and make it twice as dangerous."

Yuri's celebratory mood was instantly deflated upon hearing this and he grew quiet and somber. "So what are we doing now? Heading into the main chamber?"

Lucas pondered the question for a moment when a sharp pain exploded in his head. He gripped the sides of his mask tightly as stars sprang into view and the entire tunnel started to spin. Yuri reached out to grab his arm but Lucas waved him away, falling to one knee to support himself. An overwhelming feeling of nausea rose in the pit of his stomach and he fought it back, trying to keep himself from vomiting.

"What's wrong?" Concern grew in Yuri's voice as he tried to reach out again to help Lucas up to his feet.

"Don't touch me, stay back!" Lucas growled as he spoke, fearful of what might be the cause for his sudden onset of symptoms. He grabbed the Geiger counter from his vest pocket and switched it on, then held it to his chest where the majority of the gelatin and black liquid had landed. The counter immediately spiked into the red zone and started clicking rapidly. Yuri's face grew pale and he stepped back, unsure of what to do next.

Thinking quickly, Lucas held the counter to a section of wall in the tunnel and confirmed that it showed low amounts of radiation. He then spread a small amount of the black liquid from his chest onto the wall with his free hand

and held the Geiger counter up again. Where the readings had previously shown a nearly radiation-free section of the wall, the counter was spiking into the red zone again. Lucas stood up shakily and turned to Yuri.

"Did any of that black shit get on you?" He held his hand up to Yuri, showing him the black liquid he was referring to. Yuri shook his head as he glanced at the Geiger counter, then back at Lucas.

"How much is on me?" Lucas turned around in the hall as Yuri raised his flashlight. The look on Yuri's face told Lucas the answer almost as soon as he said it.

"You're covered, Lucas. It's all over your arms, your legs and your chest. Your mask looks pretty much clear, but the rest of you is coated with it."

Lucas nodded grimly and put his Geiger counter back into his vest. "Back up more. You don't want to get this stuff on you." Yuri quickly retreated back down the hall, away from Lucas and the passageway that was coated in the radioactive liquid. Lucas walked a few paces toward Yuri and stopped, leaning his SVD up against the wall of the passageway.

"You're sure my mask is clean?" Lucas twisted his head again and Yuri nodded, too stunned to speak.

"Good." Lucas unbuckled his right glove and pulled it off, raising his hand away from his sleeve to avoid coating it with the black liquid. He reached back to his mask and released the catch on the back, feeling it slide forward on his head as he loosened it up. Once he removed the straps, he pulled the mask off and tossed it toward Yuri, who instinctively caught it and then dropped it to the ground in surprise.

Lucas's dark hair was glistening with sweat from exertion and he rubbed his face with his ungloved hand, glad to be free from the restrictive confinement. Yuri slowly picked up the mask again and looked it over, amazed by the amount of circuitry and wiring inside. Lucas stepped back from Yuri as he looked down at his body again, shaking his head at how much of the black liquid was present.

"Don't you need this?" Yuri held out the mask for Lucas.

"No. Now it's your turn to wear it. The mask won't protect you from radioactive contamination on your skin, but most of the stuff in Prip'Yat is in the dirt and dust. This should keep you safe from most of the hotspots as you run back to your car."

Yuri shook his head firmly. "We've had this conversation too many times already. I'm going with you."

"Yuri, shut the hell up and listen to me." Free of the mask, Lucas's voice was louder than he had intended. Yuri stopped speaking and stared at him.

"This black stuff is killing me. I'm already dead. Even if I got to a decontamination chamber now, I'd die within a few weeks." As if to purposefully emphasize this point, Lucas grimaced and gripped his head as another wave of pain washed over him. "I'm in the early stages of severe radiation poisoning. Whatever this is, it came from that thing when I shot it. I'm committed to this now."

"So am I!" Yuri protested.

Lucas nodded and made a circular motion with his hand. "Yes you are, but not in the way you think. Turn over the mask and look on the side." Yuri flipped the mask around in his hands until he was looking at the interior again.

"Now you see that little indent next to the left earpiece? If you push that in and twist, it'll eject the memory chip for the mask's monitoring system. Don't do it now, though. Eject it once you're clear of the city."

Yuri brushed his finger over the indent and examined it as he spoke. "Monitoring system?"

"The mask has an integrated camera that looks out the front, along with an audio recorder. All of the data is saved to the mask's memory chip for post-operational analysis."

"I don't understand... why did you give me this?"

Lucas smiled through another wave of pain. "Two men died here tonight and the bodies of hundreds more are in the lake outside this complex. I'd bet there are even more inside the reactor chamber or wherever this thing calls home around here.

"If both of us die tonight, no one will ever know about what happened here. Even if a recovery team finds the memory chip, they'll just hide it away. The only way to make sure people know what happened is if you take the chip and distribute its contents."

Yuri sputtered in response. "But my cousin! That thing killed him! I have to destroy it!"

"There are bigger things at stake here than your cousin's death, Yuri." Lucas's voice was warm, though it cut straight to Yuri's heart like a knife. "What about those other people? What about Iosif? Who's going to make sure people know what happened to them? This isn't something that can stay hidden. This is the second creature that we know about. If there are more out there, we can't let our governments hide them from the world."

Lucas was preparing to physically intimidate Yuri in order to convince him to leave until he heard Yuri's next statement.

"Okay, I'll do it. How do I get out of here?"

Chapter Twenty-Five
Lucas Pokrov | Yuri Volkov

Lucas winced as he stepped into the reactor chamber. Without the benefit of his mask, he could feel and taste the radiation almost immediately. The flavor of heavy metals danced on his tongue as he tried not to think about the incredible amount of damage that his body was taking in addition to the damage already done by the black liquid. He moved as quickly as he could in the chamber, trying to stay one step ahead of the creature that pursued him. Venturing directly into the heart of reactor number four wasn't Lucas's original plan, but invading the creature's inner sanctum was the best way he could think of to ensure that the beast came directly to him and left Yuri alone.

After he had convinced Yuri to leave, Lucas followed him for half a mile down through the passages and watched him running across the power plant construction yard toward Prip'Yat before descending back down into the tunnel system. He told Yuri that this was for his own protection, but in reality he wanted to make sure that the young man followed through on his commitment and didn't try to come back and help him. Lucas removed the wheel from the hatch before moving back into the tunnel system, ensuring that Yuri wouldn't be able to get back in even if he had a change of heart.

Before they parted ways, Lucas left Yuri with explicit instructions on what he should do. *"Run through the city and don't stop for anything until you reach your car. Remove the memory chip from the mask and then throw the mask and your shoes away before you get in the vehicle. If you're interrogated by the military, tell them that you were going to meet a girl near the city but you heard an explosion and decided to call the whole thing off. Wait forty-eight hours and then get the information from that chip to every news source on the planet."*

Yuri had expressed significant concerns over whether or not he would be attacked by the creature, but Lucas assured him that the chances of that happening were extremely remote. Lucas wasn't completely convinced of this himself, but given that he was the one covered in radiation and had hurt the beast, he hoped that it would hunt him instead of going after Yuri. *Besides*, he thought, *that thing is probably nursing its wounds somewhere close by.* If he could find the beast while it rested, he had high hopes of killing it before succumbing to the radiation poisoning that was ravaging his body. *No better place to look than the reactor chamber full of delicious radiation.*

Lucas held the cylinder in his right hand, keeping his thumb near the trigger mechanism. In his left hand he held his SVD, keeping it at a ready position to distract the beast once it appeared. Lucas could feel his muscles ache more with each passing moment in the chamber and the nauseous feelings in his stomach continued to build. At the level of radiation in the chamber, Lucas knew that he would soon succumb to more symptoms of radiation poisoning. Nausea and vomiting would simply be the start of a quick process that would result in his death within a few hours or less.

"Of course, I'm not going to make it that long, am I?" Lucas spoke loudly in the chamber, trying to draw the creature in towards him. His voice sounded odd in his ears without his mask on, though he was thankful that he would be able to hear his natural voice before he died. Sitting down on a pile of rubble, Lucas swept his SVD around the room, trying to find the beast he was sure was nearby.

The high amounts of radiation in the chamber wreaked havoc with his scopes, though, rendering them useless in the dark room. Lucas shook his head and laughed as he raised the SVD and fired a shot in a random direction. It impacted off a wall, causing the room to shudder from the vibration. A snarl followed the vibration and Lucas immediately stopped laughing. He dropped the SVD by his side and pulled out his flashlight, directing it to the location where the snarl originated.

A large black shadow crawled along the wall of the chamber twenty feet off of the ground. The single red eye of the beast watched Lucas as it moved across the wall, keeping its distance from its foe. Never before had the creature faced an opponent that had successfully wounded it to such a large degree, and it kept a respectful distance from the soldier. Lucas stepped away from his SVD and held his hands high in the air, hovering his thumb over the trigger mechanism for the cylinder. He smiled coldly at the beast as he spoke, his voice dripping with hatred and anger.

"Well come on! What are you waiting for? Come and kill me!"

The shadow continued to move across the wall, watching Lucas as he wandering around, tracking the movement of the creature with his flashlight.

Lucas felt a spasm in his stomach and nearly doubled over in pain. He began to cough as vomit rose unbidden in his throat, bubbling to the surface and overflowing onto the piles of metal and concrete in the chamber. He felt flushed as well, and a headache that started in the back of his head was traveling to the front, settling behind his eyes. Lucas struggled to stay upright as he wiped the vomit from the corner of his mouth.

Desperate to provoke a reaction from the creature, Lucas picked up a small piece of rubble and lobbed it at the beast. It impacted on the wall of the chamber just above the creature's head and bounced to the ground. The shadow's body shook as it snarled at Lucas, then it came to a halt on the wall. Lucas threw another piece of rubble, this time hitting the creature directly in the head. Though the rubble didn't do any actual damage, the beast snarled louder and began to quickly descend from the wall. It approached Lucas slowly as it closed the gap toward him. Though it had been provoked by Lucas's actions, it was still wary of his intentions, particularly since it was not used to having its prey stand up to it in such a manner.

The beast stepped down off of the wall of the chamber and stood staring at Lucas, sniffing the air. Unable to know the exact range of the device he held, Lucas resolved to hold out on using it until the last possible second. His body continued to shudder and he felt his temperature rise as his fever worsened. His vision began to blur from the headache and he had to struggle to remain upright against the onslaught.

The beast slowly began to circle around Lucas, drawing closer, but still acting warily. Lucas saw its single eye swivel to look him over from foot to head, then it appeared to be staring directly at the device in his hand. Upon seeing the device, the beast stopped dead in its tracks and smelled the air again, then it began to back slowly away toward the wall. Shocked by this, Lucas looked at the device himself as he realized that the creature must have figured out what it was.

But how? The only possible reason for the creature knowing what the cylinder was is if this was the very same creature that Iosif and his team had encountered in China. *They didn't kill it. That's why the explosives were added. The field just weakened it so that it appeared to die.*

"How the hell did you get from China to Ukraine?" Lucas spoke again, distracting the creature from looking at the cylinder. As it trained its eye on

Lucas, he lowered his arm and slipped the cylinder into his back vest pocket. He reached into another and pulled out a grenade and held it aloft. Lucas screamed at the shadow as he pulled the pin on the grenade with his thumb and then lobbed it in the general direction of the creature. The beast leapt onto the wall, scurrying high out of range of the grenade as it bounced along and exploded, showering the chamber with dust and metal fragments.

In the confusion, Lucas reached back into his vest and pulled the cylinder back out and held it behind his back out of view of the creature. Seconds ticked past as the creature divided its attention between Lucas and the remnants of the grenade. "Come on you sorry bastard, take the bait..." Lucas muttered to himself under his breath. His request was granted just a moment later when the beast began to descend the wall again with its mouth open as it bared its teeth at Lucas in a manner eerily reminiscent of a demented smile.

That's it, keep on coming. The creature's claws tapped on the rubble as it moved toward Lucas at a steady pace. Even in the glow of the flashlight, the creature appeared completely black in color, with no patterning or texture to be seen beyond the faint outline of fur across its body. For all intents and purposes, it appeared to be a shadow, albeit a shadow with substance, form and deadly intentions.

A wave of pain hit Lucas in his gut and he fell to his knees, coughing and choking as vomit once again came forth from his mouth. He looked up at the creature, now only twenty feet from him, and struggled to his feet again. Lucas's hand slipped as he pushed himself up and his flashlight tumbled away, rolling away down a slope in the chamber. Lucas tried to ignore the pain in his chest and stomach as he stood again, facing the creature who now appeared only as a red eye moving steadily closer toward him.

When the eye finally stopped moving, Lucas could swear that he heard the creature's breath just inches away from his face. A deep rumble came from directly in front of Lucas, and he knew then that the beast was no more than an arm's length away. Lucas brought his arm around from his back, revealing the small glowing lights on the surface of the cylinder. The beast's eye widened as it noticed the cylinder in Lucas's hand, then it snarled and began its leap forward to attack. Before the creature could move more than a few inches, though, Lucas shoved his thumb into the indent on the top of the cylinder as he closed his eyes and whispered.

"This is for Iosif."

Chapter Twenty-Six
Yuri Volkov

A mile away, running through the woods as the faintest rays of sunlight began to break over the horizon, Yuri stumbled and fell to the ground as the thunderous explosion echoed across Prip'Yat and the surrounding area. Yuri closed his eyes tightly, trying not to imagine what Lucas's final moments must have been like.

Now safely away from any radiation hotspots, Yuri pulled off the mask that Lucas had given him. He threw the rubber boot liners to the side and turned the mask over. On the inside of the mask, near the left ear speaker, he found the small indentation again. He pushed the indentation and twisted his finger, rotating the mechanism and freeing a small slot to open. Inside the slot sat a memory chip no larger than a thumbnail, painted black with gold connectors at one end.

Yuri slowly pulled the memory chip out of the slot, rotating it in his fingers as he stared at it. It contained the entire video and audio log of Lucas's mission, from the camera and microphone embedded in his mask. The only proof of what had occurred at Prip'Yat was contained on the chip, a fact he found difficult to comprehend.

Once he eventually got back home, he wasn't sure what he would tell his parents or his aunt. His appearance was disheveled and he was covered in dirt and cuts, though that was the least of his worries. His sole focus was on getting the information on the memory chip out to the world, no matter the cost. If he couldn't stay and help Lucas avenge Dimitri's death, he would have to ensure that the world knew of Lucas's sacrifice along with the atrocities committed by the shadowy beast.

Obeying Lucas's instructions, Yuri hurled the mask as far away as he could, watching as it bounced down a hill into a group of trees and brush. He did the same with each of his shoes, doing his best to touch them as little as possible during the process. After retrieving a bottle of water from the trunk of the car and using it to rinse off his hands, Yuri climbed into the driver's seat and gripped the wheel, taking a moment to catch his breath before he started the engine.

A bright light appeared in the sky and Yuri shaded his eyes, surprised that dawn had arrived so quickly. When he lowered his hand, though, he saw that the light was not from the sun, but from the spotlight of a helicopter, one of a dozen that were flying toward Prip'Yat and Chernobyl. One of the helicopters had broken off from the main group and was headed toward him and the sound of the rotors soon filled the air, along with a stern voice speaking through a bullhorn.

"Step out of the car now! Keep your hands high and do not reach for a weapon!"

Yuri gulped and slipped the memory chip under the rubber lining of his car's cup holder before he stepped out of the car. *Showtime,* he thought. Obeying the order from the helicopter he slowly raised his hands above his head and did his best to put on the face of someone who was shocked to be faced with a military helicopter in the wee hours of the morning. The helicopter landed a short distance from Yuri's car and two soldiers in standard camouflage gear stepped out and ran toward him, keeping their rifles low but at the ready.

One of the soldiers spoke harshly while the other circled his car with a Geiger counter. "Who are you? Why are you here? Were you in the city?"

Yuri stammered purposefully, blinking in the bright lights of the helicopter. "Wh-what? I'm Yuri! Please don't hurt me! P-please! I'm just here to meet my girlfriend!"

The soldier rolled his eyes and stepped back to confer with his partner. "What do the readings show?"

The soldier with the Geiger counter pointed at the device. "Everything looks okay. He's higher than he should be, though."

The soldier who had been addressing Yuri approached him again, glancing down at his shoeless feet. "How long have you been out here? Where are your shoes?"

Yuri thought quickly and began stammering again. "Oh no, you're going to kill me aren't you? I just wanted to try a little bit of the stuff before she got here! I was walking out in the grass and took off my shoes and just wandered around some! Please don't kill me!" Though Yuri had never used recreational drugs before, many of his schoolmates had, and he did his best to emulate their after-school behavior as he spoke.

The soldier addressing Yuri shook his head disapprovingly and was about to say something else when his radio squawked. "All units to the plant! Code red!" Upon hearing this message he looked at his companion who nodded at him and started to head for the helicopter. The soldier spoke to Yuri again as he backed away. "Get the hell out of here, junkie! And stop coming out here or the radiation will eat you alive!"

Yuri felt a wave of relief wash over him as he nodded in response. The soldier followed his partner back on board the helicopter which took off and banked steeply away toward the power plant. Yuri stood and stared at the helicopter until it was a speck in the distance before coming to his senses. He jumped back in the car, dug the keys out from underneath the seat where Dimitri had stored them and jammed them in the ignition. As he drove down the field and out toward the road back to his home, he pulled the memory chip out and held it aloft, clutching it in his hand like it was made of pure gold.

Chapter Twenty-Seven
Epilogue
Excerpts transcribed from selected BBC news broadcasts

Three days after the event at Chernobyl
"New information is coming to us tonight from the ghost city of Prip'Yat which, as you may recall, suffered from a reported earthquake three days ago. Reports indicate that this tremor was not actually an earthquake, but was the result of the detonation of a high explosives device inside the sarcophagus at the abandoned Chernobyl nuclear power plant. We are working to confirm this report with our journalists in the field."

Four days after the event at Chernobyl
"Military-grade video footage provided to us from an anonymous source shows us the astonishing tale of an entire covert operations mission that took place inside Chernobyl and the neighboring town of Prip'Yat. Multiple independent analysts have confirmed that said video footage, which is widely available on the internet at this time, is not a forgery, though the contents of said video are both disturbing and gruesome. The video and audio shows a team of two Russian covert operations agents moving into the Ukrainian city of Prip'Yat on a mission to investigate reports of a disturbance in the area. We have compiled a series of clips from this video to give you a brief summary of the mission, but we must warn you that this footage is extremely graphic."

Eight days after the event at Chernobyl
"Thus far, attempts to find the only presumed survivor of the mission, a civilian youth known only as 'Yuri' have failed. Family members of Yuri have come forward to say that their son vanished in the middle of the night, and they are unsure whether he ran away to avoid media attention or whether he was taken in for interrogation by government officials. Attempts to get comments from officials within the Russian and Ukrainian governments have been met with silence. This is undoubtedly due in part to the strain both governments are feeling as they scramble to contain the public relations disaster and mass hysteria that has unfolded."

Twenty-five days after the events at Chernobyl
"Independent research teams have been dispatched to Chernobyl in an attempt to study the environment of what is now being referred to as 'The Beast of Chernobyl' in an effort to understand the origin of this new species. Environmental groups have also seized upon the beast as a symbol for their movements, denouncing nuclear energy as the food source for what they call 'an abomination on the earth.' Said groups in countries across the globe are pushing for independent investigation of their country's nuclear weapons stockpiles and power plants to determine whether the creature discovered at Chernobyl was an isolated case, or the beginning of a trend."

Four months after the events at Chernobyl
"The BBC is working to investigate reports of disturbances at nuclear facilities throughout the UK and Western Europe. We have been working with colleagues and reporters in the field in several other countries who have experienced similar disturbances and we will bring you updates as soon as we have them. For now, we urge our viewers and listeners to remain calm, continue your routines and avoid panic."

Thank you for reading Prip'Yat!

To view other books from Mike Kraus, please visit
www.mikekrausbooks.com
www.facebook.com/MikeKrausBooks

Email the author at
mike@mikekrausbooks.com

Printed in Great Britain
by Amazon